S0-BNT-293

Someday is Today

A Collection of Short Fiction by
Aaron Kemp

ISBN: 0-9762224-2-6

Published by Acacia Publishing, Inc.
1366 East Thomas Road, Suite 305
Phoenix, Arizona 85014

Printed in Canada

Contents

Pick Apples 1

Pharo's Army Drowned 7
    Preface 8
    Chapter 1 11
    Chapter 2 14
    Chapter 3 16
    Chapter 4 20
    Chapter 5 23
    Chapter 6 31

Someday is Today 35
    Chapter 1 35
    Chapter 2 40
    Chapter 3 42
    Chapter 4 67
    Chapter 5 71
    Chapter 6 75

Ritchie 79

Youngblood of the Grand Rhon **121**
    Book II: The Short End 171

Where Treasures are Found **179**
    Chapter 1 179
    Chapter 2 183
    Chapter 3 196
    Chapter 4 216
    Chapter 5 231
    Chapter 6 251
    Chapter 7 259
    Chapter 8 272
    Chapter 9 276
    Chapter 10 278

Pick Apples

The young man walked slowly down the dusty path between the apple trees dragging his toes in the dust. He stopped at the edge of the orchard by the dirt road that went along the irrigation canal. He looked around and quickly chose a spot under the shade of a small apple tree. He sat down cross-legged in the grass, leaned his head against the tree, adjusted his straw hat down over his forehead to shield his eyes from the sun. He was dressed befitting his job as an apple picker. He had a long-sleeved gray shirt buttoned at the wrists but opened down to his belt. His hairless chest was the color of leather and shiny with sweat. The shirt was old and threadbare, stained at the armpits and collar with sweat, and with apple leaves and bark here and there on them as well. He wore equally faded and threadbare jeans cut off just above the ankles. His bare feet were pushed into cheap black tennis shoes with Velcro straps that were always loose. He carried a small canvas bag with his lunch and a bottle of water inside. After sitting quietly, squinting into the sun, he opened his bag took a swallow of the warm water and leaned back again without taking out his sandwich wrapped in wax paper, or the Snickers candy bar, partially melted and soft from the heat.

The old man came then, down the same path, stumbling through the dust with a perpetual smile on his weathered face. He brushed some grass aside and sat in the shade of the next tree, facing away from the young man. He looked warm but not tired and moved quickly for a man of his apparent age. He removed his straw hat and ran his fingers through his ample white hair. He removed the bandana from around his neck, soaked it in the water he carried in his jug and wiped his face, forehead and hair. Without looking at the younger man, he spoke with a melodious Mexican accent.

"*Qué tal?*" He asked kindly.

"Hello, Pete," said the young man quietly. "It's too hot today."

The old man did not respond but rubbed his gray whisker stubbled face with his wet bandana, put his sombrero by his side and leaned against his tree.

He gazed skyward at the blue, blue sky with puffy white clouds, clouds that were not moving at all and looked like they had been painted there by a skillful artist with a soft brush. His soft smile never left his face as if that, too, had been painted there. He rubbed his hands together and it made the sound like adobe bricks being rubbed together. His knuckles were large and knobby and his finger joints enlarged with some fingers a little cracked. Constant dirt had left the many creases in his skin stained forever. The backs of his hands were red and brown like shiny Mexican tile.

"My fingers are getting a little stiff," he said. "Sometimes I cannot straighten them out all the way. That's from crabbing apples for 60 years I suppose."

He studied his hands for a moment.

"They do not hurt at all. Anyways, they are still good to use at least to pick apples," he added matter of factly. He then rustled his large hands through a small knapsac and brought out flour tortilla stuffed with beans and wrapped in waxed paper safe from the sun. He leaned forward, resting his elbows on his knees, took a large bite and began to chew. Glancing at the young man, a trace of concern appeared on his expressive face. Without looking back but instead studying the clouds, he spoke again quietly.

"Where is your sister?" he asked.

The young man stirred uneasily in the grass.

"She is gone."

"Where did she go?"

"She ran off with that guy — that driver — the big boy buck that has been hanging around her." His dislike was not hidden.

"Uh-oh," said the old man like he was sorry he asked.

"Christ-sake, she was just seventeen and I bet that cavrone is at least 30. Probably already married. They are on some long haul to California. Some little sister." His unhappy voice faded.

The old man squirmed to find a more comfortable position against the tree.

"I did not see your father here today?" He asked rather than stated the words, leaving it open ended, in the air.

"He was not here today," said the boy quietly. "He is in the jail in Yakima. They are going to send him back to Mexico. And you know what — he says he is glad to be going back home. That's where my mother is, in Chihuahua. He told me he misses her too much. He says he wants to go home," the boy repeated. "Home is a word I hardly know. So, you have a home, old Pete? Do you want to go home to Mexico?"

Again the old man did not answer. The painted smile was gone and his face was just blank, absent of any emotion. He looked to the right and left, up through his branches at the sky, then down at his shoes before he spoke.

"What happened in Yakima?" he asked, again without looking directly at the young man (who now appeared to be just a boy).

"My father drank a lot of rum. He felt pretty bad when Linda ran off with that truck driver — asshole. He got into a little scuffle in a bar, over nothing at all. I saw him. He acted loco. When the police came, they just wanted to send him home, but he swore at them in Spanish and ended up pushing one of the guys in the chest. The police did not even look mad. They just put handcuffs on him and took him off to the jail. They were actually nice to him really, considering. I got the camper keys from him at the jail. This morning they told me they were sending him back."

The boy looked like he wanted to bawl, so the old man did not look in his direction.

After what seemed like a long time in the noonday sun, under an apple tree with the irrigation ditch streaming by and the clouds painted onto the sky, with mourning doves sweeping past, and a restless wind first starting to rustle the leaves and grass, the old man pulled himself slowly to his feet and walked a few feet on to the road and began kicking little meaningless dust clouds.

The boy looked up and asked with wonder so clear in his voice.

"Did you leave a home in Mexico? Would you want to go back there? What is a home anyhow? I never had one, that's for sure."

Muchacho, I never left anything there except dry heat, hard work dust and poorness. Sleeping on corncob mattresses filled with bed bugs and chasing goats and sheep through cactus looking for grass. I swam the Río Grande four times before I was 12. Until I figured out how not to get caught. I cut cotton in McAllen, Texas before I was fifteen, but it was better than Mexico. I have cut asparagus, picked onions, cherries, and apples, lots of apples. I have bucked bales in the sun and bent my back in the potato fields. All of it was better than Mexico. No, I never left a home there and I have had none here either. My wife is dead and my children have grown up and live in the city. They have a home. I do not have a home except the picker's shacks they let us stay in sometimes."

He walked in small circles with a cloudy look on his face. Then stopped, put his hands on his hips and the smile returned. "I have enough to eat and a warm place to sleep; pretty soon I am going to get a dog to keep me company at night." With this he chuckled.

The boy looked at the old man in wonder.

"Is that what it is going to be like for me? What shall I do, old man? What can I do?"

With this, old man Pete went over and picked up his sombrero, adjusted it on his head and smiled through the branches again at the clouds painted on the sky. He bent down to get his knapsack and started off.

"What to do? What to do? Pick apples!" he said then walked away without looking back.

Pharo's Army Drowned

If they are deceived who flatter themselves that the ignorant and debased have no conception of the magnitude of his wrongs, they are deceived who imagine that he arises from his knees with back lacerated and bleeding, cherishing only a spirit of meekness and forgiveness. A day may come — it will come, if his prayer is heard — a terrible day of vengeance, when the master in his town will cry in vain for mercy.

Northrop Solomon
Twelve Years as a Slave
Buffalo: Miller, Orton & Mulligan
1854

Preface

To be a slave in the 17 and 18 hundreds in the southern United States was to be sentenced to a term in hell. The labor in the hot southern sun was intensive and without end. Poorly clothed, poorly fed, with living conditions that were indescribably wretched, slaves were owned like chattel. Animals were treated better. Slaves were often beaten into submission, deprived of creature comfort, half-starved by being given diets which were lacking in the most basic nutrient requirements of man. They lived in squalor and dirt, in mud and wind and rain and often cold, as well as the merciless blazing sun. Barefoot and threadbare, they labored in their masters' fields until they could labor no more, then were discarded like crippled dogs.

As bad as these parts were, the hideous humiliation and profound lack of empathy, let alone sympathy, was the slave's daily treatment. In some places, Virginia for instance, breeding farms existed where women were forced to bear seven children or more, which were taken from them at the age of two to be sold on the auction block. No amount of crying and wailing ever helped. Many times, mothers smothered their babies to keep them from the horrible fate that lay ahead. Some whites probably fought with their conscience, but they usually lost. It was forbidden to teach a slave to read or count. Girls at puberty were subjected to sexual use by the overseers, slave traders, and even the plantation owners who professed to be devout Christians. The slaves were preached at by white preachers who read passages from the Bible, exclaiming that slaves must mind their masters, submit to all or go to a fiery hell that was more like the insane ravings of a maniac than anything else.

What of the human spirit of these people? Most of time it was broken, but not always. The moving Negro spirituals were evidence of that. When Thomas Jefferson declared all men are created equal, he decreed that Negroes were only five-eights human. The absurd arithmetic of breeding with whites notwithstanding. One quarter, one half, one eighth? Where did they land?

The fact that slaves were required to maintain the beautiful old "Southern" way of life was a thought that could not be flushed from their assessment of reality. Of late, it has been popular to say that slavery was not the main issue of the great Civil War that befell our nation. It was the germ cell. It was the unabashed, undiluted, bottom line cause, pure and simple. The grotesque death of hundreds of thousands of American lives is thought by some to be God's punishment. That seems hard to question. It is only by His grace our nation was allowed to continue. Racial equality is our every present aim and is still a long way off.

So, were their slaves just always complacent? Did revolts and slave resistance occur? Yes, they did. Over 100,000 slaves escaped to Canada. Many hundreds went to live with various Indian tribes in Oklahoma and elsewhere. Their descendents are there still.

Did not the slave people live with hate, distrust, and often not well hidden disgust, engendered by whites? They did, and in Watts, Chicago, Harlem and Louisiana, Mississippi, Georgia, Alabama and many place it continues. It seems that revenge has not occurred much at all. Not much at all. Considering.

Negro slaves were the craftsmen of the South. They were the furniture makers, carpenters, brick makers, and farmers. When white slave owners saw their successes it frightened them and brought on many more excesses of cruelty and subjugation.

Again, many, not a few, went forward against all odds to smuggle families to the Quakers and other abolitionists of the North.

Occasionally, one man was pushed too far. One man tired of hanging his head and bending his back. One man would tolerate no more outrage against his person and those he loves.

Such a man was this man named Tomas.

Chapter 1

It was dusk, but still hot when the big Negro slave Tomas trudged his way up the twisted, poorly marked, almost hidden trail that led to the hill looking down on the pond. It wasn't exactly a pond but backwater from the Green River that swelled with murky tide water. What resulted was a pond twelve feet deep and fifty yards or less across, depending on how much tide water was trapped. A shelf of granite was usually exposed on the opposite side from the hill. Aligators lay there almost all day absorbing the sun. They stayed so still that they looked like logs.

The top of the hill was Tomas' spot. His place. This is where he came to watch the sun go down. When he was a young man, perhaps in his twenties (he didn't know his age), this is where he crawled to when they cut off half his foot for trying to run away. As he sat down on a stump, he remembered the terrible pain. It took several chops with a hatchet. He had told himself that he wouldn't scream or cry. In his agony and disbelief he screamed and…cried. While the caretaker wrapped the remaining foot in a tight rag that immediately became soaked, he did not swoon. He wished he could. He did not faint. He did not die. He wished he could. An old woman and an old man dragged him off to their cabin where they gave him some whiskey they had hidden away. It didn't help, but the kindness did. He remembered it all so well. His stump still hurt him, particularly before it broke open and drained again. As he sat, he lit up his corncob pipe and looked down at the stump of a foot in a cut off boot. At the time, he swore he would kill the man. He had not forgotten and he knew that someday he *would* kill him. He swore it again now in a whisper.

When it got dark and the moon came up, he could see the gators, huge gators, swimming about, leaving moonlit trails of ripples in the water. They were ugly and he feared them. Someone had told him once that the cut off part of his foot was thrown in there.

Sometimes he slept right there on top of the hill wrapped in two dirty blankets he kept there. He would get up early and wait with the other slaves by the water pump well until Massah Park came with the daily orders. Massah Park, an ugly, balding, bulging, whiskered man, rode a black horse and carried a short bullwhip. Always carried a short bull whip and wore a pistol of some size in his waist holster. He grinned when he talked and gave orders like a barking dog. They all hated him. They were all wildly afraid of his smallest displeasure, let alone his wrath.

But today Tomas had to go back. Cora from the kitchen slaves had food for him but more she had let it be known she urgently wanted to talk with him. So, down he came, glancing back at the moon on the water and the evening breeze in the leafy trees. His foot hurt more going downhill and he had to be careful about stumbling.

He found Cora waiting for him behind the smoke house. He loved her like a daughter. She had been the wife of his old friend Tobias and when they shipped him on down south, he swore to keep and protect her as best he could. He never had a wife of his own. Somehow, because of the foot — the cut — he could no longer be a man anyway. Sometimes he cared, but not often. Now, she needed something, he thought.

"Tomas, problem," Cora said with a choke deep in her throat.

"What, chile?"

"That bad man Massah Park, he looking at my little girl Elsie. He look at her that way. She just a little girl, thirteen. Oh, Tomas, we have all seen it before when that happen. Tomas, not my Elsie. Not my Elsie," and she began to cry into the bandana she had in her hand. Tomas said nothing but took the quaking woman in his arms for comfort. His black eyes glared like a cat's into the night. His brow wrinkled, but his lips snarled silently. She felt the strength of the shoulders, the hands, and the arms.

"Gotta do sumpthin', Tomas. Gotta protect her. Gotta do something," she groaned.

"Yeh, we do, and we will," said Tomas holding her tightly.

Chapter 2

Across the river at another south Georgia plantation, further inland, a slave in his twenties crept out
of his cabin in the darkness. He carried an old flour
bag with all his paltry belongings. At his belt in a
crudely made sheath of pigskin, he carried a knife
that he had painstakingly fashioned from an old file.
His shoes were made of sack cloth with leather soles
he had fashioned from an old harness. He moved
quickly, apprehensively, alert but not frightened. He
had told no one he was running away. For a fleeting
moment, he felt a twinge of loneliness. It passed and
he continued on to the river where he had hidden a
small canoe that he had fashioned from a log using a
picture from a book he had found. He wanted to see
Tomas. He needed advice. He didn't know stars or
how to keep from being tracked down by the dogs.
He knew about Tomas's foot, painfully knew, and he
had no intention of letting such a thing happen to
him. He paddled across the river as fast as he could,
moved the canoe upstream and hid it by sinking it
with rocks, waded a good mile down stream in water
about his ankles, then pulled himself out on a limb.
The trees were big here and he had no trouble going
from limb to limb, leaving no tracks and no scent on
the ground. He progressed in this fashion until he
came to a rocky ledge six feet above the ground. He
came down on the ridge of it and let himself down
the other side causing no disturbance in the rocks.
He found his cave entrance in the dark, ducked

under and let himself into a small room where he had stored odds and ends he thought he might need — rope, a blanket, a threadbare hand-me-down jacket, fishing line and hooks, a fork and spoon and a handful of Lucifer matches. In the morning he would be missed. In the afternoon, dogs would come. Now, he would be safe. In two days, he would go find Tomas by waiting for him at his place on the hill overlooking the pond. For now, Lenny felt safe enough.

Chapter 3

Elsie and her mother lived in a one room cabin near the big house. It had been that way for as long as she could remember. When she was five years old, her father, known as Hugh, was taken from them and sold on down south to Louisiana. Vaguely, she could remember her mother's anguish and pleading tears which had changed nothing. The tears and anguish were worse when Cora learned that Hugh had tried to run away back to them. He was captured and whipped so severely that he died when the whip dug a hole into his shiny chest and his lung collapsed. Cora was taken to work in the big house in the kitchen, as well as scrubbing and changing, emptying the chamber pots, washing clothes and chopping wood. Cora learned how to make herself as unattractive and ragged as possible. She learned how to absolutely avoid being along with the massah or his hired overseer. Even with any of the other unattached male slaves. She practiced talking goofy, like she was simple and out of her mind. She did a good job of it, and she was protected. Part of the time, Elsie was with her but more often was left alone or ran into Sarah Jane, the daughter of the plantation owner, who fed little Elsie stolen cakes and bread from the kitchen under the big magnolia tree in the back yard.

"What's her name?" Sarah Jane asked.

"Her name is Elsie, miss," answered Cora. "She's my daughter."

"How old is she?"

"I don't knows numbers," she lied (she knew). "Someone told me she be eight years."

"That's how old I am," sighed Sarah Jane. "Can she play with me?"

"Sure thing, if you mother say."

The next day, Sarah Jane found them under the same tree during lunch time.

"My mother says it is all right. She gave me a lot of rules, but it is all right anyhow. Come on, Elsie, I'll show you my room."

Elsie had said nothing. Her eyes were wide with apprehension. She looked like she wanted to cry, but she followed along slowly, looking back at her mother repeatedly.

"I'll be in the kitchen right after the dinner bell. You come."

I hope good can come of this, she thought.

Elsie and Sarah Jane became friends despite the differences between them. Sarah Jane gave her little orders sometimes like a slave master, but not often and increasingly less. In addition, they were always reasonable and kindly-stated orders. After awhile, Elsie just ignored orders, but then after awhile, she just said no. Sometimes. Not too loud. A major thing was that Sarah Jane very patiently and carefully coached Elsie in her language and taught her to read. Elsie learned very fast and after awhile it wasn't clear who was teaching who. These lessons they kept secret because they knew it was against the rules. They were very careful to keep the secret. Very careful, because they knew that Elsie would be taken away if anyone found out. Sarah Jane had to take piano lessons twice a week from the preacher's wife. Sarah Jane hated them and only practiced when threatened by her mother. Elsie sat obediently and silently in the near corner, watching and learning the piano herself. The piano was in a separate little room off the hallway. When it was practice time, the girls would close the doors. Sarah Jane's mother could hear the practice and rejoiced in the nice progress, little guessing that most of the time it was Elsie on the piano stool. The girls loved the joke.

Time went on and the girls grew. Once, Sarah Jane invited Elsie to eat with them.

"That is simply not done in this house," said her mother sternly. Her father glared at her, then looked to his wife, issuing unspoken orders to put an end to these ideas!

They grew to twelve, nearly thirteen, and their bodies began the mysterious changes. Elsie became a foot taller than Sarah Jane and the soft balls on her chest became pointed. Her hips became round. She walked different. Her waist became slim and she cared about cleaning her face and shining her teeth. Sarah was smaller but right behind. When their first "sweet secret" occurred, it was about the same time. They had both been told at least something about what to expect between the legs. They were a little frightened at first.

Cora tried to keep Elsie's chest wrapped so her breasts didn't show, but it helped little. And Elsie would unwrap when she became uncomfortable. She saw the older boys and men looking. She saw the overseer looking, and it filled Cora with a dark, sickening dread. When Sara Jane was sent to boarding school in Atlanta, Elsie was given a job on the kitchen staff; at least she was not sent to the fields.

The entire group of household slaves stood in a line outside the big house as Sarah Jane was put into a buggy. She was crying piteously but quietly, as was her mother, who didn't want her to go. Elsie watched from by her mother's side calmly sniffling quietly.

"Bye, Elsie. I'll wri...." She stopped herself.

With that, the team pranced away from the waving folks at the big house.

Chapter 4

When the horsemen and dogs came through everyone knew that they were looking for an escaped slave. The slaves from Merryweather plantation where Tomas was tried very hard to pay no attention and avoid eye contact with the searchers. After watering their horses and rounding up their hounds, they were gone.

"Who?" one of the hands asked Tomas without looking at him.

"Lenny," Tomas said under his breath without looking at him either.

That evening, just at dark, Tomas make his way to his place on the hill. He carried a bag this time, slung over his shoulder. He stood still listening. There was a soft whistle behind him that was supposed to sound like a bird.

Without moving a muscle, "That don't sound like no bird I ever heard." said Tomas, "Come on out, Lenny."

Lenny stepped out from the shadows into the scant moonlight.

"Diddy, doo, Tomas."

"What that mean?"

"Hello," said Lenny with a smile in his voice.

"Hello," he answered. He was now looking in Lenny's face. "They come by with the hounds today, but they couldn't catch nothin' this side of the river. I heard 'em say they thought you floated on down. I think they wanted us to hear that. We has got to be careful." he added. Then after a pause, "How long you been gone?"

He held up three fingers "This will be night tree."

Tomas sat down on his stump and pulled out two corncob pipes and a pouch of tobacco. He motioned for the insecure man to get onto a log across from him, gave him a pipe, and, after filling his own pipe, the tobacco. "You keep," he said.

"Thank ya," said Lenny with gratitude expressed in a short glance.

"I bring ya provisions in that sack there."

"That was good of ya. I hungry all right," said Lenny.

"Eat. We have to get a plan. I know one thing, you can't move out for at least a week or more or they will hunt you down. Stay hid careful."

"You got a plan, Tomas?" asked Lenny.

"No," Tomas said sharply. "Who's 'scapen? Me or you?

They sat quietly puffing their pipes for awhile.

"I'll get a plan." Tomas said rising. "You stay hid good. Make the food last two days."

Tomas began his way down the trail awkwardly because of his foot.

"Tomas?"

Tomas turned around from the waist up.

"Tomas, you come with me."

"Can't do that, Lenny. Two get caught. 'Sides, I too slow, you got to be fast. And, and I got somethin' to do." He was proud of the word.

"Tomas."

"Yes?"

"Thank you with all of inside me."

"You welcome with all inside of me, but you ain't clear away yet."

Tomas hobbled down the trail, not looking back.

Chapter 5

A week later, the tobacco crop was all bundled up and packed in wagons to take to the auction. They were last spring's rapidly growing broad leaves, picked, rather than cut, in their prime and hung to dry upside down in the sheds. They were turned frequently and wiped free of dust as they went from to green to brownish yellow and developed aroma that make a smoker's mouth water. It was like a festival occasion as they pulled out early in the morning. Overseer Park drove the lead wagon. Two others followed, driven by the owner Mr. Merryweather and Tomas in the last wagon. These were large wagons, each pulled slowly and methodically by two grand sized oxen. It would take all day and into the evening to get to the auction the next day. The auction would take most of that day, and by afternoon they would be heading back. They would make better time returning so would be home at 9 pm when it was still light. This was the plan, every year, and it worked well. Merryweather would have a satchel of cash under his wagon seat, a double barrel shotgun with buckshot across his waist. Both he and Park had a brace of pistols around their waist.

Tomas noticed that Park was taking frequent swigs from a demijohn of whiskey he kept under his seat. He drank a lot but hid it well. All knew to stay away from him at such times, because he was mean; mean and hateful. Mean and ugly as a snake. By the time they returned, Tomas knew the whiskey was gone and Park soon would be looking for more. For some reason it worried Tomas, and he worked as fast as he could to release the oxen in their pen. All the time he watched. That is when the idea, the plan, came to him.

Master Merryweather carried the satchel of money into his office while Park lugged in the shotgun and the extra clothes they had brought. They left the door open so Tomas could see them roll the rug back and open a trap door in the floor where the satchel was placed. The door closed, then the trap door locked shut. A small desk was placed over the lump in the carpet where the lock was, and everything was back to normal. As the lantern was extinguished and the door closed, the plan grew.

Big Tomas watched as Park half-staggered to his quarters behind the barn. He lit a lantern, pulled off his coat, and as Tomas watched from the shadows, Park brought out another bottle of whiskey and started slurping.

Time to get ready. He knew what was coming up.

The big black man walked into the barn, ducking under the windows light so he wouldn't be seen. He talked quietly to the black horse and got a handful of grain for him. He saddled him up with the plantation saddle and kept the bridle around the barn, He might not have time. He left the barn area and waited in the shadows beside the cabin. He didn't have to wait long. The drunken man swaggered out of his cabin like he was in a hurry and beat it over to the door.

"Open up, nigger. Open up, ya hear?" He didn't wait, but kicked the door in.

"You, Cora, Get outta here," Tomas heard the slur in his menacing voice.

Don't fight him Cora, thought Tomas.

"No." He heard Cora say. "Please no mo' sah. Please no. She just a little girl," Cora plead and cried as she was thrown out the door.

"You want to watch?" he snarled with a hideous laugh.

Cora got to her feet and was starting back in when she felt Tomas' hand on her arm. She stopped then and looked at him, the fear gone from her intense face.

Inside, they heard. "All right girl, get that dress off you. I want to see you all naked. I want to show you somethin' you will learn to like from the boss man."

He didn't hear the footsteps behind him as he began fumbling with his belt.

A strong arm wrapped around the man's neck and lifted him off the floor as the other hand pulled the pistol from his halter.

The white man struggled fruitlessly and the big arm tightened and held.

In a time, the struggle stopped. Tomas squeezed some more then let the frame slip to the floor. Quickly he pulled his arms behind him and wrapped the two wrists together with bailing wire he had brought for the purpose. He tightened, twisted, and tightened again until the fingers couldn't move. He made a figure eight loop around the knees allowing them to be six inches apart so he could walk when the time came. Tomas rolled Park over roughly as he was coming to. As Park opened his mouth to yell, Tomas packed a filthy rag from the stable, lubricated with manure into the gapping mouth. He packed it in as far as he could with the barrel of the pistol then tied another rag around his head holding the gag in place.

Then he jerked the smaller man to his feet.

"We goin' for a walk" he said, as he half dragged him to the door. "Is it all quiet out there Cora? Any lights on?"

"No, Tomas, all dark" Elsie stood wide-eyed against her mother.

"Go on in, fix the door." Tomas said as he pulled the reluctant assailant. They did as instructed.

Tomas pushed, kicked, pulled, and jerked Park up the trail. He had to place a rope around his neck to yank him along. Finally, they reached the top. Park's eyes were bulging and rolling in his head.

"You 'member when you cut off my foot?" Tomas stated rather than asked. He drew his long knife from his belt and methodically cut all of Park's clothes off. The slave driver's fright was in his eyes. He was limp as a rag and did not, or could not, resist.

"Now, I cut somethin off of you."

He grabbed the man's penis and sawed it off. The blood shot out.

"The gators like blood," Tomas whispered in his ear.

With that, he kicked the feet out from under Park and rolled him over the edge into the murky pond He watched with unfeeling eyes as the gators came and began their hungry rolling dance as they tore the body to bite-sized bites to suit a gator.

Tomas watched for a while not knowing what he felt. He did not know what, but there was no regret. He gathered up the clothes, then kicked the dirt up all around to hide any blood. He brushed the area all with a branch and followed his tracks down the trail brushing away any sign of passage. He walked as quickly as he could. He must complete his plan this night.

Tomas went to the office adjoining the big house where he knew the trap door was under the rug. He had little trouble opening the door with a screwdriver and, being quiet as possible, he let himself in, moved the desk, rolled up the rug and inspected the trap door latch and lock. In a moment he could see how to remove the hinged latch. He went to the black smith shop and returned with the nail cutter used to cut the horseshoe nails. He worked the pincher around the head of each nail in the latch. Cut them quickly, then simply lifted the latch free. He reached inside without being able to see and came out with the satchel and the money.

Back at the barn, he brought out the black horse after bridling him. He tightened the girth, then tied the satchel up behind the saddle with the saddle straps. He then brought the animal out to the hitching rack and tied him loosely.

He went to the overseer's cabin and found a carpetbag. He stuffed clothes and belongings of all kinds into the bag and brought it back with him to the horse. He carried out the clothes that he had cut off the man, tied them into a ball, put a rope around them to drag from the saddle. The horse spooked a little as Tomas led him away because of the bundle dragging behind it. It was like something chasing him. Tomas did not know how to ride well, (no practice for that slave), but he understood mules and animals, so had little problem settling him down and walking off down the road dragging the bundle on the ground.

It was three miles to the edge of the river and the group of heavy trees where Lenny was hiding. It took him an hour to get there. Tomas held the horse and whistled like a bird several times. Presently he heard rustling in the brush.

"Tomas?" A whisper.

"Yes, come here."

Lenny looked at the horse wide-eyed and filled with question.

"You take this horse now, and get, ya hear. You ride good, don't you?"

"Oh ya, I ride." said Lenny eagerly.

Tomas held Lenny's foot, and he bounced into the saddle and took up the reigns.

"See this rope tied to the bundle of clothes?" Lenny nodded. "The dogs will be following the scent trail. You ride fast tonight, then bury them things deep or sink em with a bunch of rocks. Don't want em ever found, ya hear?"

"Somethin else, Lenny"

Tomas reached up and took the satchel off and opened it.

"Lots of money here." Lenny looked barely believing. Tomas reached in grabbed a handful and put the bills in his own shirt. "The rest be yours."

Lenny sat on the horse without speaking, He watched as Tomas reattached the satchel to the back of the saddle.

"You know which way is south and north?" Tomas asked.

"Yes, I do. I got a compass."

"Well I'll be!" exclaimed Tomas. "You go south two days or so. You hit a big road that go both way. Don't go north until you get to dat road. Then, nobody can follow you. Gather up what you need from your cave. Den, get out of here. Remember; ride fast through the night then get rid of the clothes being drug. The dogs won't follow you no more then. Dogs can't tell one horse smell from another so be sure there are other horses there where you ditch them things."

"All right Tomas. Just like you say. I do just like you say. Thank you. Bless you. Thank you."

As Tomas walked away, he looked back over his shoulder.

"Good luck man." he said. "Get goin'."

Being sure he left no footprints (he again wiped them out with a branch), he made it back to the plantation.

The carpetbag was where he left it by the barn. He dug a hole by the manure pile, placed it in and covered it with four feet of manure.

"Now, let them come." he said out loud. The money in his shirt was hidden in the rafter of the barn. Not until then did the big man go to his bunk and collapse. He slept until daylight came in through his open door.

Chapter 6

It was the routine of the plantation that a honk on a conch shell trumpet brought the slaves to the center of the yard where they awaited their daily work orders. When no honk was heard, the slaves came anyway. Slowly, looking confused, they squatted on the ground talking quietly to each other in hushed wondering tones.

No massah overseer. Confused, the slaves, men and women, began to mill around looking.

"What in tarnation is goin' on here?" shouted the big boss as he walked out of the big house spinning around and around to look in all directions.

"Where is Park?" he shouted. Of course, no one answered, making the plantation owner frustrated and angry.

"Drunk, that's what," he said as he briskly walked to the overseer's quarters.

The door was open. He went in with a course stomping on the board floor. He came out again directly shouting.

"He is gone. He is, damn it, gone. His stuff is gone." He sounded confused and bewildered.

"Did anyone see him go?" he shouted at the gathered slaves with their heads hanging down, idly kicking at the dirt. Of course, there was no response.

The desperate appearing man raced to the barn threw open the door and walked a few steps in.

"His horse is gone!" The owner stood for a short time. "Damn," he bellowed. "What the hell?" A look of part understanding came over his face and he turned and darted to the office. He saw that the door was sprung open there and when he looked inside he shrieked when he saw the rug rolled back and the trap door gapping open. He did not bother to look down the hole. He spun around with his fists clenched in the air racing to the big house.

"Sarah Lou, Sarah Lou. We have to get the sheriff over here." Turning his head fitfully, "Tomas, hook the mare to the carriage and be fast about it," he screamed.

Tomas hurried to do as he was instructed. Shortly, the stomping, sweating, overweight, red-faced man came out carrying a shotgun. Tomas attempted to help him into the carriage but the old man pushed him aside and whistled and whipped the fat little mare into a reluctant run down the road. He went cursing all the while.

It was only two hours before he was back with the sheriff, three armed deputies and a skinny black man being drug by three hounds.

The deputies, the sheriff and the owner, still jumping around talked loudly.

"He won't get far. We'll catch up with him," the sheriff said reassuringly. The deputies nodded their heads with a knowing reassurance of their own.

"Bring me a scent cloth or something from his place."

A used towel and an old sock were brought out and stuffed under the dog's noses.

"Get!" yelled the dog handler, which the animals did with their famous enthusiasm for the chase. They howled and barked vigorously and took off down the road following the scent trail.

The mounted horsemen, the sheriff and the deputies trotted after them leaving the hapless dog handler to run along behind.

"Get my money back and kill that son of a bitch!" shrieked the not so dignified big massah. He stomped into the house where the missus was waiting, looking horrified as she held the door.

Tomas put the carriage and mare away like nothing had happened. He almost strangled to keep from laughing. The slaves looked happy as they went about their individual business.

"My plan work." said Tomas to himself. "They aren't gonna catch nobody.

"Go like hell, Lenny. Good luck."

Someday is Today

Chapter 1

Discontent comes sneaking through the cracks of a man's life at uncertain and unexpected times. A myriad of things bring on the unwanted feelings of anxiety and restlessness that open the fissures. Perhaps they can be put back, stuffed away, postponed, but the feelings cannot be ignored for long. Discontent hangs on through every effort to end it with reason or judgment. Hangs on and grows worse with efforts to disengage it from consciousness. Frustration results from attempts to avoid the discomfort malcontent causes. Discontent should not be confused with boredom. Boredom is a man-made feeling, like guilt is. Boredom is the product of lack of imagination. Often is, anyway.

How many times had he found himself daydreaming about what he was going to do someday? Someday? When was someday, anyhow?

Dr. Mickovich, known to all as plain "Mick" or "Doc," was confused by his discontent. He was 62 years old, a successful general surgeon and general practitioner from a small, but pleasant town in rural California. He lived with his 21-year-old son when he was not away at college. He had a small but comfortable ranch in the foothills above Salinas, one hundred and twenty-five acres of irrigated pasture, a few cows, pallid Herefords, and four nice Mustang-Arabian horses that he enjoyed riding, training and just watching. His practice was busy and successful. At age 60 he was excused from emergency room call, so his time was reasonably predictable. His office hours were four days a week and he did the surgery that interested him and was not too demanding. He was financially secure, with stocks and annuities that guaranteed him more comfort than he ever dreamed of as a young man starting out.

Five years before, breast cancer had taken his wife of 40 years. The hollow place that had been left inside him gradually filled in with comfortable memories and hopeful anticipation of future happiness and purpose. These things came close for him, but never completely moved in. Very gradually, optimism faded, and he became more matter-of-fact than he would like to be.

His two children had done and were doing well. His daughter Jean finished teacher's college, had married well and was expecting her second child. His son Clark was in the fourth year of pre-med. His grades were good despite a slow start and a wild time to begin with in college. He had a good chance of getting into medical school somewhere, even if it was in Mexico. He shaped up when Mick refused to give him any more money. He worked his own way through then, working as a deck hand on his Uncle Vito's fishing boat out of Pedro. He had a lot of pride and Mick was proud of him. His father let him know that he had put aside money for medical school for him if he could get there. There was no doubt he would accept that.

Mick had had a close relationship with Linda for three years now, but he could hardly call it a romance. At least he couldn't even if she did. Weekends in Vegas and San Diego, a cruise through the Panama Canal, and two weeks in Tahiti had solidified nothing. He wondered if he was capable of loving her the way she wanted him to do. He had no one else and liked being with her. He even thought about her a lot, but he just didn't know.

Things came to a head after Clark came home at the end of winter quarter. He seemed pensive and preoccupied, which fit so well with Mick's mood at the time. After several abortive efforts to draw him out, Clark somewhat tearfully announced that he didn't know what he wanted to do. He was not going back for spring quarter. He was not happy with the prospect of medical school and the hours of dedicated studies. He was not sure he wanted to be a doctor. He did not know what he wanted "for Christ's sake." It was easy for Mick to understand. He was disappointed though, as a matter of fact.

"I am sure you have given it a whole lot of thought, Clark. What have you come up with?" asked Mick in a fatherly way.

"I want to run Vito's boat," he replied. "I've got some ideas about going deeper and identifying different species before we set on them. I mean, going after Petrel Sole rather than filling up with Dover or Black Cod and Yellow Eye rather than Rock Cod that are too small and getting smaller." Clark fidgeted, "And," he hesitated, "and I wonder if you could see your way clear to give me the money you set aside for medical school to get the gear?" He looked intently at his father with a hint of pleading in his eyes. "I'll pay you back," he added. "Vito has already said he wants to give me the *Hooker*. Just plain give it to me. His two girls don't want it and his son is a busy lawyer who hates fishing anyway."

Mick looked out the window, at the ceiling, at the floor, at his shoes, at his hands.

"Just give it to you?" he asked.

"Yes, for one dollar. There's something else, Dad," he went on. "I want to write. I really want to be a writer." There was a long uncomfortable pause. "I'll have lots of time with the boat on autopilot with the net out." The young man smiled. They both smiled.

Mick stood up, walked around the silent room, then turned to his son who was looking apprehensive and intense.

"All right, Clark, we'll do it."

"Don't you have to think about it Dad? I mean this is great, but…."

"Nope. One condition."

"What?"

"I am going with you!"

"You're going fishing?"

"Yes. You and I are going fishing on Vito's boat. Someday is today."

"What?" asked Clark.

"Never mind," replied Doc.

Chapter 2

Plans were made rapidly. Dr. Mick, with Clark, arranged for a Locum Tenens to come to his office three days a week. His receptionist and billing clerk would stay on as long as they were needed. His office nurse was happy to work just three days a week. He could come back if he wanted to or needed to and take up where he left off. For the first time in a long while he found himself humming and whistling and even singing out loud. He made a dinner date with Linda. He was eager to tell her and wished she would share his enthusiasm. The date did not go well at all.

Linda was late. Unusual. She sat down and ordered a Bloody Mary. Also unusual. She began talking after first planting a platonic kiss on the bald spot of his head.

After the usual "how are you's" and pleasant-ries, she began to address him with earnest restraint.

"Mick, the bank wants to promote me to Manag-ing Director. This a Vice President position."

"Well, that's wonderful, Linda." Linda looked like it wasn't all that wonderful. "Isn't it?" Mick asked in a confused way.

"They would have to transfer me to San Diego," she said flatly, searchingly.

"Oh," said Mick twisting his water glass with obvious discomfort. She said nothing.

"When?" he asked.

"Thirty days," she replied.

Mick felt anxiety tugging at him. So many things were changing. They ate their lunch, or rather picked at it, in silence.

Chapter 3

Red opened the sliding, sticky galley door and stepped onto the deck. Immediately he noticed the breeze on his whiskered cheek, beet-red and sensitive from the sun. The breeze, though slight, was cool, too cool. Rather than being constant, steady, it was intermittent and for an instant or two, now and then brisk. Automatically, he looked around the horizon. It was not yet dusk, but the sea birds were winging toward the shore. Not in any formation. Not in a hurry, but at a constant rate. Not looking back or crying to one another. At a constant altitude, never diving into the sea head first after bait fish or stopping to rest, bobbing up and down as they seemed to love to do on incessant waves. It was warm still and humid — sweat beads did not leave his brow and his shirt clung to his back and underarms as he went up the ladder, over the bridge and into the wheelhouse.

He poked a finger repeatedly on the barometer glass and the needle fell four full units. He looked again at the horizon, this time only to the west. About five miles away he could see another vessel disappearing and reappearing like some magic trick, in his view.

That's those shitheads, he though to himself. *They followed us out here because we know where to fish.* There was some satisfaction to him with this thought. They only followed high-liners, not rust bucket half-assed scows. He wrinkled his brow as he squinted at the horizon. *The swell is building*, he thought. Perhaps 8 or 10 miles away, directly to the west, he could see clouds gathering with billowing fingers pointing skyward. Large, he could tell, white thunderheads. He took the wheel from his son Ted, with a gentle but direct shove.

"Go down and get your dinner and straighten up the galley. We have to get the net aboard pretty soon."

Ted glanced at his father inquisitively.

"It's only been about one hour, Dad."

Without looking at his son, Red answered matter-of-factly. "We're in for a blow. Get moving."

Ted looked at the horizon and saw the clouds to the west. "Yep," was all he said as he left for the galley. He felt stupid for not noticing them himself.

Red's boys, Ted and Steve, were good fishermen and good sailors in their own right. They could navigate and steer with, against or forty-five degrees into a swell and hold a course within a few degrees, spinning or slowly moving the large wheel just enough each time. They could mend nets very fast, both of them, splice line and cable using a fid or marlin spike with skill and ease. They knew the names of all the myriad of fish species they caught and within a penny or two, the going price per pound at the cannery. They were sailors. They had respect for the ocean, the weather, the wind and the sea. And for their father.

Steve, the older, 27 now, had quit school in the 10th grade at age 16 to fish full time with his father when he first acquired the *Charm*. Ted followed suit two years later in the same grade. They had all worked hard refitting, painting, repairing and re-everything so that now the 52-foot boat was thought to be the best of all its class in California. She could handle a storm, but a true sailor hates a storm. Ted and Steve were apprehensive as they put everything away in the galley, fastening the drawers and doors shut as they did.

In less than a half hour's time they were through, standing on deck looking to the west. The boat was rolling now from port to starboard with an irregular rhythm that was difficult to anticipate and therefore made it difficult to stand. If you look at a sailor on deck, he is constantly standing with his legs wide apart and, if possible, holding onto whatever is stable. After many years of this, they do the same thing on shore out of habit. Also, their knees are never locked but are like automatic hinges to go up and down with the roll of the sea, so are constantly bent a few degrees. They stood there holding on, broad-based, pulling their gear on over their rubber boots.

Red slowed the boat to a two-knot crawl, keeping the bow turned at 45-degrees into the mounting swell.

"Okay, start her in," he yelled out the pilot house door at his two boys on the deck. Steve pushed the big dog tender forward and with a soft moan of protest, the cable began to slowly come in, laid out in perfect rows by the level wind. The cable was 9/16-inch stainless, capable of holding and pulling 30,000 pounds. It was painstakingly manufactured in Coos Bay, Oregon, where the magnificent winches were also made, the best and strongest available, and used by fishing vessels around the world. When a wave hit the stern, the stretched cable sang like a twanged banjo string. If one broke, a man's head would likely go flying into the ocean like a beach ball. Dangerous work. The storm made it more so.

The wind, at first just a little cooler than usual, was cold now and coming constantly at 9 knots with short gusts of 12 to 15. It whistled through the rigging and blew the small flags into flapping frenzy. The clouds had finished forming and covered the sky with grayness, blowing amorphously from west to east. The ceiling was no more than 700 feet. Off in the distance, sheets of dry lightning bit the sky. The crew waited patiently, waiting for the huge doors to break the surface. Doors are flat metal or heavy wood structures designed to hold the net mouth open, scooping the fish in. They weigh 500 pounds or more. When they are brought up from the depths, they swing out to the side on additional cables supported and managed by large double blocks as they are shouldered into their resting positions on each side of the stern. They are very heavy and this can be difficult anytime. When the sea is rough it is more difficult and dangerous.

At last the two came up, breaking the stormy surface together. The winches, lightened as the surface tension was broken, began to turn faster until the doors were swinging in the air.

The pull of the heavy net leveled the boat against the swell at first, but then with the stern held down, the bow began to swing from side to side with the waves. It was difficult for the captain to hold the course, and he cursed softly to himself with the struggle. The heavy doors were brought alongside as the vessel pitched crazily with the swell and pitch. The leaden doors came in unevenly, with the port about three feet behind the starboard. The port side was left dangling on its cable as the port winch was shut down, allowing the starboard one to catch up. Ted was watching over his shoulder at the starboard side as his side was allowed to land over the side.

"Hey, for God's sake, pull that port door up and make it fast!"

His warning came too late. The boat lurched over because of the sudden pull made worse by the port oncoming sea. In an instant, the huge metal heavy door lurched over the gunnels and struck Ted on his chest, in the back under his arm with a sickening crunch. Ted was knocked off his feet and thrown like a rag doll across the deck. He lay moaning pitifully.

Red paused for a second looking down at the scene. "For Christ's sake!" he screamed.

Immediately he switched on the autopilot and then darted down the stairs to the deck. "Shut off that winch and help me over here," he yelled at his other son who immediately did as he was ordered. Together they wrestled the door around, backed the heavy cables and lashed the door into place, secure.

"Get the other one up."

"All right." Steve started the starboard winch again and when it was alongside, they secured it, moving and reaching, pulling and straining with the roll of the deck. When it was secure, without a word, Steve started the net reel and began winding the net aboard. Ted had not moved. He lay with his face against the deck, breathing with difficulty, apprehensive and in pain.

Red stood over him then and took him under the arms and lifted him gently to his feet.

"Are you all right, boy?"

"No," said Ted, swallowing a painful cough. "My ribs are broken. I can feel them crunching. I'm hurt bad, Dad."

"Bullshit! Get up to the wheelhouse and keep her on course while we get the fuckin' cod in."

Ted held onto the bulkhead as he made his way over to the ladder and crawled up onto the flying bridge. He was silent but his face was distorted and twisted with pain. With effort he slid the door open and fell into the wheelhouse, resting against the wheel. The pain in his chest was excruciating and he felt dizzy and sick. Now he felt his stomach beginning to ache, constant but intermittently severe. Nausea overcame him until he was forced to vomit out the porthole. Staggering back, he slumped on the floor behind the wheel, unable to hold his head up as black fog settled over his eyes. Just before he fainted, an uncontrollable cough overcame him. He felt a warm, frothy blood spew between his lips and run down his chin.

The net was reeled into the cod-end which was packed full with 10,000 pounds of bottom fish.

Working quickly, Steve and Red strapped the sack filled with fish aboard, spilling them into the holders on deck. With the net aboard, the boat floated more easily on the waves, rolling into the trough between the swells.

Steve looked pleadingly at his father standing on deck with his hands on his hips up to his knees in fish. He looked angry, red-faced and upset.

"Ted is hurt bad, Dad."

"Oh, bullshit. He just cracked a rib."

Almost reluctantly, he left the deck, climbed the stairs to the flying bridge and made his way along the pitching flying bridge deck to the wheelhouse.

"What a hell of a mess," he exclaimed with resignation.

He was not prepared for the sight in the wheelhouse, and it horrified him. Ted was slumped on his side on the floor with bloody sputum and dry vomit on his face. He was ashen white and wet with sweat. At first Red thought his son was dead, and he felt turmoil in his heart.

"Steve! Steve!" he yelled.

Gently he lifted his son up to the bunk on the aft wall of the wheelhouse.

Steve, aware of the desperate tone in his father's voice, ran to the wheelhouse as fast as possible.

"Oh God, Dad. What do we do?"

"Get on the horn. Call the Coast Guard. Tell them we need a doctor fast."

Steve took the radio in his trembling hand, flipped it on the automatic energy channel.

"Calling the Coast Guard. Calling the Coast Guard. This is M.V. *Charm* calling the Coast Guard. May Day. May Day."

The radio squeaked and crackled.

"This is the Coast Guard, Point Hieden back to the *Charm*. Please advise. Are you sinking and in immediate danger?"

"No, no, we have a severely injured man aboard. We need a doctor immediately."

"What is your position *Charm*?"

"Loran lines 15795 and 60392."

"What are the weather conditions?"

"Twenty-foot seas, 10 or 15-knot winds. It would take two or three hours to get ashore."

"Man, we can't get a chopper out there now. There is a storm and it's dark as hell. What is happening with the injured seaman? We will ask a medic to advise you."

Red flew across the wheelhouse and grabbed the mike from Steve.

"Listen to me, you," he yelled. "This is my son. He needs help! He was hit in the chest with a seven-cawl door. Do you know what that is? It weighs half a ton. He is coughing up blood. He needs help or he is going to die. He is not a fucking seaman. He's my son. Now you get a chopper out here!"

There was a pause as the radio crackled.

"Stand by *Charm*," said the Coast Guard voice.

"Stand by my ass," Red yelled into the mike.

He dropped the mike dangling on its cord and returned to his son.

"Ted, open your eyes, can you?"

Slowly Ted's eyelids fluttered open.

"Dad, oh God, my side, my belly, I hurt. I'm dying. Help me."

Red wiped the moisture from his cheeks and brought the blanket over his son awkwardly and gently. The big man felt for his son's pulse. It was rapid and weak. He could hardly feel it. He felt panic overtaking his reason.

"Dad, how about that doctor on the *Rose*?" He let his sentence drop.

Red stood up slowly and walked over to the microphone stiffly.

"Calling the Coast Guard. *Charm*."

"*Charm*, this is the Coast Guard. This is Medic Daniels. Describe the patient's condition."

"Shit," exclaimed Red. "He's in terrible pain in his chest and belly. He hasn't got a pulse. He's spitting up blood and puking."

"Have you got a first aid box?"

"Yes, but all it has are some bandages and aspirin and shit."

"Don't give him any morphine. He's probably in shock."

"Morphine? I haven't got any morphine."

"Have you got any I.V. fluids?"

"What the hell are you talking about? I haven't got anything like that."

"Keep him covered and as warm as possible. He's probably in shock."

"Covered and warm! Probably in shock! You silly shit, he's dying. Now you get a chopper out here now!"

There was a long pause. Then the laconic reply:

"Weather conditions won't permit. With daylight... maybe a chance.... Bad storm."

Ted moaned and coughed.

"Dad, he needs a doctor," Steve said with determination. If you don't call the *Sea Rose*, I am."

Red stood looking at the radio. Steve reached for the mike but the big fisherman pulled it away from him. He dialed the selector knob to the hail channel and spoke evenly into the phone.

"*Sea Rose, Sea Rose, Sea Rose*, this is *Charm*, come in...please. Red closed his eyes. "Please, God," he whispered.

"This is *Sea Rose* back to call." The voice was clear and inquisitive.

"Is the Doctor aboard?"

"Yes, this is the Doctor. Is there some problem? What is the matter?"

"Doc, my son, he got hurt, hit by a door. He's hurt bad. Can you help me?"

There was another long pause and Red was about to yell into the mike again when the box spoke.

"What's happening with him? Where was he hit?"

"In the left side of his chest in the back. His ribs are broke. I can feel them move. He hurts like hell. He coughs and blood is in his spit.

"Does he have abdominal pain?"

"What?"

"Does his belly hurt?"

"Yes, and it's swelling up. His pulse is really fast and weak, Doc."

"All right, *Charm*, I am coming over. Did you call the Coast Guard?"

"Fuck yes, but they can't help in this storm. Some shit-hell medic…"

"Yeah, we're only a mile or so to your west. I can see your lights, I think. Switch your mast light off and on. Yeah, *Charm*, I have you. Coming full speed. Hold on."

Red let the mike drop on its cord.

"God, hurry," he muttered.

The *Charm* pitched and rolled in automatically to the swell trough. The fishermen turned the bow into the waves and turned the engine up to 2700 RPMs, heading for the lights to the west that he knew was the *Sea Rose*. Ted rolled over slowly onto his left side while Steve held his hand.

Aboard the *Sea Rose,* they had just finished sorting their catch into the fish bins, only 2,000 pounds, when they heard the call. Clark, seasick to death, was leaning over the rail vomiting again and again. He was too sick to remove his oilskins and go below. Besides, the cool breeze on his cheeks gave him his only comfort.

"Someone is calling on the radio," Doc said to himself as he turned the bow toward harbor.

After the conversation he put the autopilot on and called Clark on deck.

"Did you hear that?"

"Yeah, Dad, I heard. You aren't going to help those assholes are you? Fuck 'em."

"You get in here, Clark, and take the wheel."

Clark did not move.

"Now, Boy!" Doc said firmly.

Clark let go of the rail, scowled at his father and went reluctantly and slowly into the wheelhouse.

"Head for that mast light."

"God, it's rough. I feel awful," Clark said.

Doc went into his stateroom and pulled his emergency medical box out from under his bunk. He opened the box and inspected its contents. There was a good supply in the emergency medical kit. He had purchased three liters of normal saline, two vials of plasma, and I.V. tubing and needles. In the medicine bottles he found vosaxyl, morphine, Benadryl and Cortisone.

"Good," Doc said to himself, "I'm going to need this stuff."

After he had closed the lid securely, he took the large box onto the deck and fastened a cloverleaf around it with a strong nylon line.

"I'll just have them swing their boom over to me, then hoist it aboard their boat," he said to himself. "I wonder how in hell I'm going to get over there."

Doc looked up at the ever-darkening sky and the first large raindrops, warm and soft, hit his cheeks. The *Sea Rose* cut easily through the swell, leaving a trail of singing foam in its wake. Doc felt a moment of apprehension. *What if the guy is so injured I can't help? God I hope not. I have to try anyway. Jesus, how am*

I going to get over to their boat in this swell and wind? He looked into the sky again and let the rain fall softly on his face.

"Jesus, be with us this night."

When the *Charm* came alongside, big Red ran over to the gunnels.

"Keep about a fathom away!" he yelled against the wind, "So they won't bang into each other."

Doc took over immediately.

"Loosen your boom, Red, and let it swing over my deck so I can get my medical equipment over there."

Red stood appraising the situation for a moment, then silently released the guy lines that controlled the boom and expertly let it swing from his boat to the *Sea Rose*. While the boats were pitching and tossing, nearly colliding, Doc took the line from the end pulley of the boom and tied it to the four loops of the clover hitch around his medical box.

"Keep going straight ahead at 3 or 4 knots," Doc yelled to his son at the wheel. "You do the same, Red."

Red did not reply, but his son yelled "Gotcha," and waved his arm out the wheelhouse window in agreement. With both vessels moving slowly at 45-degrees to the waves, they were stable enough so that Red could winch the boom back to his vessel and lower the bag carefully to the deck.

"Good," yelled Doc. "Now untie it and send the boom back to me."

"Are you crazy, Dad? You're going to try and swing over there.?"

"You got any other ideas? Should I jump?"

The boy flipped on the autopilot and started to come aft.

"Damn you," Doc said, "Get back in there and steer."

Just then the *Sea Rose* was lifted suddenly by an extra large wave that sent it crashing into the side of the *Charm*. Doc said nothing more, but the boy raced obediently to the wheel and quickly got control of his boat.

Presently, Red managed to swing the boom over the deck of the *Rose* again. Doc took the hook of the line through the end block, pulled enough slack, then snapped it in a snug loop around his waist. He reached over his head and took a tight grip on the line.

"Red, can you get me pulled up and over there? Can you hold me?"

"I can hold you," he answered.

With all his might and strength, Red pulled on his end of the line and lifted Doc off the deck a foot. He did this with one powerful arm and with his other arm he began to swing the boom back to the vessel. The effort was tremendous and the process seemed to be working well until Doc put one foot on the bulkhead of the *Charm*. At that time both boats were hit by a large, rolling wave which was breaking into windblown froth on the top. Both boats lurched and dodged crazily. Red held on with all strength, sweat rolling down his face, eyes bulging with the effort. There was nothing for Doc to do but hang on, and hang on he did until his hands ached. He swung past 3 or 4 feet, then back in again, but could not get over the side. His foot slipped off again and he dangled precariously between the boats. A wave, again bigger than most, suddenly uplifted the *Sea Rose* and slammed it hard into *Charm*. Red saw what was happening and pulled Doc up as hard as his muscles and weight could do. With the roll of the *Charm*, then by some way, Doc was over the deck of her. Red released the line at that moment and Doc crashed to the deck in a heap. Red released all hold on the boom and simply let it go as he ran over to Doc. He reached down and grabbed him under the arms just as the wildly swinging boom caught up with the rope around Doc's waist. It pulled him suddenly to the side, and for a moment, there was a tug-o'-war with Red holding on to Doc, and the rope from the swinging boom pulling him toward the side.

"Undo the damn line before it squeezes the shit out of me!" Doc said with quiet desperation. Between Doc and Red, they managed to unsnap the swivel, releasing the line from Doc.

The two men stood for a moment on the pitching deck, panting and relieved.

"If I knew you were going to drop me like that, I would have worn a parachute."

"Sorry, man." Then, "You have to come see my son quick. He is bad hurt." There was pleading torment in the big man's voice.

Doc took a step toward the wheelhouse steps and fell forward on his hands as his ankle gave way with a nauseating surge of searing pain. He could feel the grind of abnormal motion of bone ends.

He stifled a cry.

"I broke my ankle. Help me up the ladder."

Big Red looked at him, then the ladder, and with a soft grunt hoisted Doc upon one round shoulder and carried him with no effort up the ladder, across the bridge and into the wheelhouse where he deposited him on the Captain's Chair.

Quickly, Doc reached over to the lad's pulse as he lay unmoving and breathing in many painful gasps.

The pulse was rapid and weak. Doc felt his brow and found it cool and moist.

"He's shocky. Get the medicine box up here fast. Cover him with a blanket. Get his boots and jacket off first." The other guy did as he was told, pulling each rubber boot off rapidly and throwing them on the floor out of the way.

"Help me with his jacket. Lift him easy."

The boy moaned and cried out pitifully as they removed his oilskin jacket. By the time Doc had his shirt unbuttoned, the boy was tucking a blanket around him.

"Raise his legs up on something too. What is your name?"

"Steve."

"Raise his legs up in the air, Steve. Put those life jackets there under them. We need to get them elevated."

Red deposited the medical equipment box onto the deck and, without speaking, opened the latches.

Doc grabbed quickly at the contents and pulled out a plastic I.V. bottle of saline. Quickly, he plugged in the I.V. tubing and let it fill, holding the bottle up with one hand as he did so.

"Hold this I.V., Steve."

Steve took it eagerly and stood holding it up as high as he could reach.

"No, not so high. Just hold it a minute."

Doc took an 18-gauge needle from the kit and placed it on the I.V. line. Then he put the blood pressure cuff on the young man's arm and pumped it up as he listened. He could barely hear the blood pressure.

"80 over 40," he said.

"What does that mean?" Red asked apprehensively.

Doc did not answer. He adjusted the blood pressure cuff to fit so the veins would fill, took the I.V. bottle from Steve and held it down below the patient and punctured his antecubital vein at the elbow. Blood came back into the tube and Doc knew he was in the vein.

"Fasten the bottle up on something high," he said as he deftly taped the needle in place. He found a Velcro fastener I.V. board in the box and attached it to the outstretched arm.

"Good," he sighed as the saline began pouring in. He opened the valve all the way and let it run in. With the I.V. running, he listened to the young man's chest. On the right side, he could hear the air moving in and out as he breathed laboriously. On the left side, he could hear ribs cracking together but no air moving. There was a strange slapping sound of the heartbeart.

"He has a bunch of broken ribs and I think he has punctured his lung." He listened intently at the apex of the lung. "He has a pneumothorax," he said.

"Christ," said Red, "What does that mean?"

Again, Doc did not answer him, but spoke to himself.

"He has a tension pneumo from the rib fracture puncturing the lung."

"Doc, what is happening?"

Doc looked up at Steve who had finished fastening the bottle to the swinging chart light.

"That's good, Steve. Start heading in at a safe speed."

"Red, do you have any medical equipment? There's no O$_2$ in this kit. Do you have an oxygen bottle?"

"Yes, there's a small one with the welder."

"Get it. Now," Doc said.

Red turned immediately and was gone out the door.

With the I.V. fluid, the young man looked better, but he was still pale and seemed to be struggling more for air.

Doc rummaged through his medical supply box, found an endotrachial tube but no laryngoscope. Again he looked desperately. No laryngoscope.

"There is no laryngoscope!" he exclaimed

"What?" Steve asked.

"I need a scope to put the endotracheal tube in his trachea. There is no fucking scope in this box!"

"What can we do?" asked Steve pleadingly.

"We'll have to do something else."

Doc thought hard. He would have to let the tension off the man's chest on the left side. With each breath in, air was leaking between the lung and the chest wall, not only slowly collapsing the lung from pressure, but forcing the heart and great vessels to the right, shifting the mediabtinum. Doc had shifted the blood pressure cuff to the other arm — 90 over 50. He glanced up at the I.V. bottle which was just about out. He changed the I.V. as soon as it was flat and out of fluid and again let it run directly for a few minutes. Then he slowed it down to a constant drip he judged to be at 200 cc/min.

"I'll just try to keep him at 90 systolic."

Steve looked at him in agreement, not knowing what he meant.

When Red put the O_2 down on the floor, Doc noticed he had cut the rubber tube so it could be used to reach the young man.

"I brought the garbage bag," Red said, producing a kitchen-size bag.

"What for?" Doc started to ask but slapped himself as he realized why.

The two men opened the bag, punctured a hole in the bottom and put the tube in it. Masking tape came out of somewhere and was used to tape the tube in place as both men fumbled together to accomplish the make-shift O_2 tent. Red opened the valve of the O_2 too fast at first, but then regulated it to a constant flow. They kept the bag filled with O_2 over his son's face and tucked it around the sides.

The boy seemed more comfortable very quickly, but still breathed laboriously and irregularly.

Doc's brow furrowed as he felt his trachea at the base of his neck.

"He has tension pneumo all right."

"Christ, Doc, what does that mean?" asked Red.

Doc explained how the leaking air was pushing the lung over as it was being collapsed, exactly like a low pressure pump with a check valve, pumping air between the wall of the chest and the lung itself.

"I need some sort of one-way...got an idea. I got an idea. Have you got any rubbers aboard?"

"What?" asked Red. "Rubbers?"

"Condoms. You got any condoms?"

"You got any, Steve?" asked Doc.

Steve hesitated a moment.

"Yeah, I have a couple in my wallet."

"Give them to him," Red said without a glance at his son.

Steve fumbled in his back pocket, pulled out his wallet and opened it up. Inside were two blue-colored rubber condoms neatly placed inside a folded sandwich baggy. He handed them to Doc saying nothing, but returning directly to the wheel.

Doc found two large-bore needles in his box, no. 14. With many silk sutures, he tied the open end of the condoms over the connecting end of the needles. Then with scissors cut a small hole in the sock end of the rubbers. He knew it would work, and he felt a little elation with the relief the knowledge afforded.

"I'm putting a hole in the cod end," he said (referring to the bag at the end of the drag net that collected the fish).

Steve and Red just looked at him blankly.

"Never mind," said Doc, "but that was pretty funny."

Doc felt the man's side and located the space between two broken ribs. There he pushed the blunt needle through into the chest at an angle, slipping over the rib above. The man winced and moaned.

"Hold still, fella. We are going to help you breathe better." There was the audible sound of air escaping out the end of the condom as he inhaled sharply. Then as he exhaled, the condom was immediately sucked shut against itself. The second needle condom valve was deftly inserted into a space above more posteriorly. They worked well. Each time the boy breathed in, his lung expanded against the air trapped in his chest, forcing it out the needle. But when he breathed out and the chest wall fell, air could not be sucked in because the rubber collapsed, forming a shutter valve.

"Praise God," Doc said to himself.

"What Doc? Is he going to be all right?"

"A wise friend of mine told me good ideas come from God, so praise God."

"What?" Red said again, then realizing what he had heard, nodded his head and said, "Yes, yeah, praise God all right."

The injured man presently became much less restless as he was able to breathe effectively. Doc felt his abdomen. It was firm and tender, slightly distended. Carefully he pushed down a few inches under the ribcage on the left.

"Does this hurt here?"

"Yes, a lot," came the muffled reply under the oxygen tent.

Doc pushed again, then released his pressure suddenly. The boy winced and moaned sharply.

"He has rebound," Doc said to himself.

He put his stethoscope on the abdomen and heard loud continuous bowel tones from irritated intestines.

"He has a ruptured spleen, I think," said Doc. "He has blood in his belly. How long until we get in do you think?"

"Two hours, Doc."

"Call the Marine Operator and contact the hospital. We need to have an ambulance waiting at the dock." He paused, "With blood available."

While Red got on the phone, Doc drew up Demerol in a small syringe and administered 50 mgm slowly into the I.V. tubing.

"That will help a lot, man. Try to relax and breathe as deeply as you can. Things are all right now. You are going to be all right."

Doc's confident tone was comforting to everyone. Even to Doc himself.

"Could you get me a bag of ice for my ankle?" he asked Steve. "My ankle is killing me."

Soon he brought the ice. Doc pulled off his boot and felt his ankle. He felt the bone on the outside of his ankle move under his finger producing a sharp pain. He stifled a gasp. He found an ace bandage and wrapped it snugly around his ankle, crossing over his joint. It felt better as he gingerly laid the bag of ice over the joint.

"Is it bad, Doc?" Red asked with concern.

"Naw. I just broke my fibula."

"Oh," said Red, not having a clue what a fibula was.

They made arrangements through the marine operator to have an ambulance meet them at the dock. For the next two hours they cruised to shore with a following sea giving them a push with each wave. Doc administered Demerol in small amounts every hour or so and kept the I.V. running at a constant rate, titrating the rate to maintain a blood pressure of 90. There were two units of plasma also, and they were given rapidly intravenously. Doc looked up from time to time and was relieved to see the *Sea Rose* following a hundred yards behind in their wake.

When they were able to see the flashing red light of the ambulance as they turned around the jetty into the harbor, the last remaining 100 ccs. of fluid was all that remained in the I.V. bag. Soon they were skillfully docking and the securing the vessel. Doc could hear the voices and scuffing of feet as the ambulance crew made their way across the flying bridge into the pilot house. They skillfully and quickly appraised the situation, and one went back to the ambulance returning with O-negative blood in a plastic bottle. He attached it with dispatch to the I.V.

"How big is the needle?" he asked.

"18-gauge," Doc answered. "It's in a big vein. Open it up. He has a ruptured spleen."

"Are you a medic?"

"He is a doctor," Red answered for him.

The ambulance driver looked inquisitively at Doc, glancing at his scruffy beard and dirty clothes.

"I make house calls," Doc said matter-of-factly.

No one seemed to get the joke.

When the blood was running in satisfactorily, they carefully and gently lifted him up out the door and onto a stretcher.

"He has needles in his left side, men, be careful with them."

The ambulance driver looked under his t-shirt, seeing the needles with the tied-on condoms.

"What the hell?!" he exclaimed.

"He has a pneumo with tension. Those are valves."

"Well, I'll be jiggered!"

"Call your hospital. Tell them to have the O.R. ready. He will need a chest tube to suction, but he can't wait too long to get that spleen taken care of. You hear?"

"Yes, doctor, will do," they said as they carried him off the boat. Obedient respect was in their voices.

Doc sat alone in the wheelhouse. Red and his other son, Steve, had ridden with the men to the hospital in the ambulance. His ankle was throbbing painfully and he felt sick with the pain. But he felt something else too. Elated and a little proud. The proud feeling was one he had felt before when he had done well as a doctor. Always he pushed it down out of consciousness. This time he let the feeling stay.

"Sometimes I can be a damn good doctor!" Then pensively to himself, "I wish I were taking out his spleen myself."

Clark appeared in the door of the wheelhouse, deep concern on his face.

"Are you all right, Dad?"

"No, I'm not. I broke my ankle!"

Doc looked up at his son, grinning. "Good job, Clark, bringing the boat in, now help me out of here. I have to go to the E.R.

Clark lifted his dad to his feet and held him around the waist.

"How is the hurt guy?"

"He is badly hurt. Punctured lung from broken ribs and a ruptured spleen." Doc paused long, "But he is going to be all right if the surgeon is any good at all. I want these stinking boots off," he added.

Chapter 4

Doc sat in a big overstuffed chair in Uncle Vito's front room. His ankle ached in the walking cast he wore. The tibia was separated from the fibula, and it required a screw to fix. He was looking at a month in plaster. Going out fishing again was out of the question. Not too secretly, he was glad. Doc's mind began to wander a bit, and he felt slightly euphoric from his pain medication. He was getting drowsy also, when the doorbell startled him to alertness.

"Come in. I am not getting up," he yelled at the door.

Red came in and walked directly into the living room.

"Hello, Doc," he said quietly.

"Ahoy," Doc answered with a grin. "How's your boy? I heard they saved his spleen. That's good. He'll be better off keeping it."

"He's going to be all right." He looked around the room self-consciously, then dropped onto the couch. "You saved his life out there, man."

"Well, I was glad we could help."

There was a long pause with neither man looking at the other at all.

"Thank you."

"You're welcome."

After another proverbial pause, Red got up and started to the door.

"I just wanted to say thank you."

"Hold on, Red. Let's have a drink of Vito's whiskey."

Doc pointed to the bar in the corner. "Pour us a drink of that Haig & Haig Pinch. I gave it to him last Christmas anyhow."

Red didn't hesitate. "Okay," he said with a bright smile, "Vito's whiskey."

The two men had a couple of drinks of Vito's whiskey and talked about the weather, politics and the fishing industry in California.

"When are you going back to doctorin'?"

"Pretty soon." Doc was surprised by how soon he answered and by his own enthusiastic reply.

After Red left, Doc sat quietly thinking about things.

God, he missed her, he really did. He could feel her presence around him.

"I think I may have made a mistake. I just hope it is not too late," he thought out loud.

As he sat there thinking, a part of the conversation returned. When Doc said most any doctor could have handled the situation as well as he, Red said, "You miss the point. You missed the whole point, Doc. The fact is, and the point is, you were there and you did. Not anyone else, you. You deserve to give yourself a pat on the back, don't you think?"

It felt good, what Red said. It felt good. In life people should be much more willing to pat themselves on the back. People who can do that never end up seeing shrinks with esteem problems and dysphoria. Monkeys do things simply because they do it well (so do most other animals). The reward they give themselves, any other reward, is really extra. He remembered seeing a famous Hollywood actor being interviewed. Why did he act, besides the money of course? Similarly, why do some actors continue to act even though they don't even make a living? It was because they like the way it felt inside to do something they could do well. That's it. The way they felt inside. Other things, applause, for instance, are extras.

His thoughts jumped again rapidly to Joy. "I have loose connections," he thought. No, there was a connection. He felt good inside being with her and simply thinking about her. For heaven's sake! He did it well, being with her. He was his best. He was more polite, kind, funny, caring, clever, considerate, and even at his best appearance with her. "My God." he thought, "I'm in love with her. Is it just because of what she does for me? How I feel?" He thought of making love with her. Many times he cared more for her enjoyment and her gratification more than his own, much more, and almost always his own were extras.

Suddenly he felt anxious and slightly panicky. He did not like the tone of things when they parted last. He wanted to talk to her now. He wanted to see her now, in person. He wanted to hold her now and tell her things. He had to get home. His mind raced. He could not drive his car with a clutch, a brake, and a gas pedal. He would take Vito's car and leave his truck. Vito's Monte Carlo was an automatic. He got his stuff together and clomped out of there in an unreasonable frenzy. He forgot to leave a note. The song from <u>Annie Get Your Gun</u>, "The Girl That I Marry," went through his mind and out his lips.

Chapter 5

When she left the restaurant, she was mad — mad, angry and confused and upset. But more, she was deeply disappointed. What's with men? What's with commitment, what's with "I'm not ready yet?" What's with "I can't be sure?" Life its very self is a risk. What do they lose? She was sure of his affection for her and absolutely sure she was the only one in his life, as he was in hers.

She went home, showered a long time in water too hot, drank two glasses of expensive Chardonnay and fell asleep reading a Jane Austen novel.

At work two weeks later she was approached by the attorney upstairs from the bank while they were alone in the elevator. Not for the first time. He was handsome, well dressed. Charming and at least five years her junior. In a way, he seemed shy. That was cute and somewhat out of character.

"Would you like to meet me for a drink or snack or something after work?" he asked with reserve.

"Do you even know my name?"

"Sure I do. It is Joy. Joy Gilbert, and you work in the bank. Do you know my name?"

"Mr. Van — something," she replied.

"Just call me Robert," he said as the door opened.

"All right, Mr. Van — Robert. I will meet you in the lobby at four."

They were both smiling widely as she walked off, leaving him on the elevator.

Joy found herself giggling inside. A date. She felt like a schoolgirl.

They walked to the Green Turtle around the corner, chatting about the weather and such, but hardly looking at each other.

"I'll call you Van, Robert. Are you married?"

"Well, no."

"Why not?"

"I don't know. I haven't had a chance lately. Are you married?"

"No."

"Why not?"

"I haven't had a chance lately."

They sat down drinking good California Merlot, getting to feel very comfortable about things. They hummed along with some of the piano player's tunes and laughed at silly observations around the room. The fake palm tree with plastic coconuts. The teenager with huge baggy pants and his cap on backward. An old lady lugging a purse as big as a suitcase. Another lady who walked by with a dog that looked just like her.

"You know what, Joy, I'm hungry. Let's get a steak or something."

"I saw a sign when we came in that said they had fresh Dorado — mahi-mahi. How about that?"

"All right, lady. You have fish. I'll have steak. I need it for my red blood cells."

They laughed together as they went into the restaurant part and were seated at a small table. They had more wine before their dinner came and were all smiles as they ate.

When they stepped out into the street, it was almost dark.

"Can I take you home?" Robert asked.

"I walk to work."

"Can I walk you home then?"

"I don't know. What are your intentions?"

"I don't have any. Just to protect a damsel."

"I am not exactly a damsel."

"That's all right. I ain't exactly a knight either."

"Come on then," said Joy taking his hand. His hand was soft and strong. His aftershave smelled sweet and manly. He was handsome. She was… was something or other. She didn't want to be alone now… or something else.

At her door he paused, asking with his eyes. She opened it with her keys, reached inside and turned on an indirect light in the hallway."

"Can I come in, or rather, may I come in?" he asked politely.

She paused only momentarily.

"Why not?"

She turned on some CD music from the '80s, brought him a glass of expensive Chardonnay and shared one herself.

"Let's dance, Van Robert."

He came to her with arms reaching in the dancing position, still holding the wine in his hand.

"Put down the wine," she said, putting hers on the table. He bent over, setting the glass on the table.

When he straightened up, they bumped into each other, paused for a moment looking at each other's eyes, then joined their lips together in a soft kiss which grew. Joy pulled back.

"Oh my," she said, then put her arms around his neck and took his lips again. Their kiss began to fill with passion. She felt his hands pull her blouse out of her skirt and felt his warm soft hands caressing slowly up her back until he was fumbling (very slightly) with her bra strap.

She felt her breasts release, then being cupped gently with soft fingers searching for her nipples. The smell of him was enrapturing. Quietly and gently he began to nudge and lead her to what he knew must be her bedroom. He was good at it. He knew what he was about.

"No," she pulled herself away. "I don't want to do this. I do, but I don't. I won't"

He looked stern.

"Please go."

"Well, I'll be damned. You a tease?"

"No, I'm not. It is not what I want. I am sorry."

"Me too, " he said as he made for the door.

"Bitch," he said as he slammed the door behind him.

Joy didn't know whether to laugh or cry, so she laughed, drank his wine, laughed again, drank her wine, then went off to her shower knowing she didn't have to go back to her bank again.

"Damn it. I love you, Mick."

She was crying gently when she turned out the light.

Chapter 6

Joy skipped off to sleep fairly easily at first, but when the quieting effect of the alcohol wore off, she was awake. Four o'clock in the morning, staring at the ceiling with water-filled eyes. The anger was gone. At least she thought it was. Maybe Mick was just not for her. Maybe just not right for her. Maybe he wasn't capable of any kind of commitment. *Men are fickle*, she thought. Some big part of them just stays little boys. But damn, she loved him. The thought made her sad and she bit her lip. *I am done crying*, she said to herself with resolve. Out of the night she heard a rapidly approaching car skidding around the corner and coming to a noisy stop in front of her apartment. Soon she heard stomping up the stairs and presently her doorbell rang. Joy sat straight up, reached for her bedside lamp, fumbled out of bed in a rush, and started for the door. She knew who was there and she was glad.

The impatient doorbell rang continuously. She peaked through the peephole and could just make out Mick's stern face peering at the door. She opened the door as far as the night chain would allow. She said nothing.

"Joy, I am here."

"I can see that," Joy said flatly.

"Can I come in?"

Without answering, Joy unlatched the chain and opened the door for him. She stepped back and considered walking away. But she didn't. She looked into his eyes quizzically. Mick limped across the room and dropped onto the couch.

"I broke my ankle."

"Yes, I see you have a cast. What happened?"

"It's a long story. I hurt myself on the boat." There was silence.

"Joy, I missed you like hell."

"Hey, romantic."

Mick stood up quickly and held his arms out and open.

Joy came over slowly. When he reached for her, she put her hands around his neck. Gently, he brought her in and kissed her softly, looking into her eyes until they closed.

They held each other then, rocking quietly in each other's arms.

"Joy, oh, Joy, I want to be with you. You are... for me. You... I feel like you are a part of me. I am incomplete without you. I want to make you happy." There was a long pause again. Mick, expecting to hear her say... say... he didn't know what.

"Joy, I want to marry you. I know it's kind of sudden. Will you marry me?" Mick was suddenly intense. He searched her eyes.

"It isn't very sudden for heaven's sake. Five years."

"Yeah, I'm a dimwit. Will you marry up with me? Please?"

"Mick, do you think you may be forgetting something? Kind of important?"

A quick look of confusion flashed across the doctor's face, then, with a smile, he understood.

"Joy, I love you. I love you. *Te amo, je t'aime, ich liebe diet, se agapo.*"

Joy smiled also and pursed her lips in a little girl fashion.

"I love you, too."

Red lights flashed through the window of the apartment. Doc let Joy go and hurried to the window. On the street a police car was pulled alongside the Monte Carlo and the patrolman was talking on his radio. Mick pulled the window open and yelled out:

"What's the matter, officer? That's my car."

"This car is stolen. You had better come down here, sir."

"I'll be damned. I should have left a note."

Dr. Mickovitch laughed out loud and kissed Joy like a husband off to work. "Are you sure you want to marry me?"

"You're not getting out of it. I'll visit you in jail!"

Ritchie

For most kids the thought of moving would create some apprehension and anxiety — even some fear of the unknown. For Ritchie, however, at age ten it seemed that a great adventure was about to begin. He lived in the city a few blocks from Greenlake. As long as he could remember he had always lived there in a big house with a cherry tree in the yard, an empty garage and an alley where a guy could play in the dirt. The garage was turned into a clubhouse by his older brother Harold, and his friends. Harold was mean and wouldn't let Ritchie or his brother Arne even go in there. Arne was eighteen months older and mother always called him "the good boy." Ritchie, on the other hand, was known as a clown, a character and a mischievous actor who brought all kinds of trouble on himself. It was Ritchie who always got caught anyway. Perhaps he was a little careless. It was Ritchie who got caught stealing oranges off the cart at the grocery store in Greenwood. Got a spankin' for it too. It was Ritchie who got Arne to steal a box of wooden matches so they could light a ball of paper afire in the paperboy's shack down the street. Caused a lot of excitement, it did. They both got spanked for that one and Arne screamed all the while that it was Ritchie, his ideas, his doings, and it was, too. When Ritchie was six, he crawled into the Model A pointing down the alley, on a hill, released the hand brake and was off on a little, very short excursion into some garbage cans piled against the neighbor's building. No spanking this time. No harm done. His old man just laughed and jokingly slugged him on the shoulder.

So now they were going to move out in the country — way out. Out of the city where horses and cows lived, out where there was a forest and a stream too. Ritchie was dizzy with the thought that maybe he could get a horse. He never did.

They arrived near the end of the school year. Ritchie and Arne were put into the same classroom filled with country kids who already knew each other. Fourth and fifth grades together with a sharp-tongued, round teacher who always seemed to be sweating off her nose, causing her to continuously be adjusting her eyeglasses. By and large she was nice, just blunt and sharp-tongued. She liked Arne a lot because he was very polite. He could read better than anyone and stayed out of trouble. Ritchie, she just wasn't sure of. She couldn't determine if he was bright or not. He was always "wool-gathering" she called it. Daydreaming. Not paying attention, and certainly not trying very hard. His wisecracks sometimes were out of control, but — my he was funny, and the teacher, Franny Burger, often found herself

laughing at him much to his pleasure and her con-
sternation and class disruption.

Ritchie had to fight a few times on the playground when the boys tried out the newcomer. He
could fight good, however, and even with bigger
boys he got a bit even if they got a sandwich. Very
soon they found that out and left him alone. Too
much alone, I am afraid. Arne had no such problem.
The biggest kid in class flipped his books out of his
hand and before they all settled on the floor, Arne
had pasted him full square in the nose and sent him
off crying to the boys' room with a very bloody nose.
Ritchie noticed that Ms. Burger had seen the whole
thing but said nothing about it at all. She just turned
and went from the hall to the classroom. It was
pretty good.

Where they lived was out a ways and a fair walk
to school. Across the cow pasture, through some
woods, and along a long dusty road with a swampy
marsh on one side which filled with water, making
good pools when it rained. In the fall, bright, strong,
green-headed Mallard ducks with bright red legs
flew out with their honking protests. In the spring,
the mother ducks just skittered out among the weeds
to their hidden nests. Soon they would be followed
by a little train of miniature quackers paddling along
trying desperately to keep up with mama. Butterflies
and brightly colored moths and bugs of all types
lived in the lacy, hanging bushes along the road with
mosquitoes galore. Chinese ring necks, beautiful
pheasants, lived on the dry islands between the cat-

tails. They were always exciting to see walking on the road or taking flight, just skimming the low trees and bushes on their way. They cackled wonderfully as they took off, protesting, or just saying, "piss on you" to whatever disturbed them. In the fall they crowed and cackled every morning to challenge the day. Quail hippity-hopped along while darting into the blackberry bushes to hide their heads and peep when people passed. When the big blackberries became ripe and juicy in late summer, the air filled with the sweet aroma of berries ready to be plucked and popped into the mouth, all warmed by the sun. Fingers became stained — like the lips and around the mouth. Arms became scratched too. Ritchie wondered why God put such awful thorns on blackberries. Maybe it was because they were so good. Good things can't be too easy to get. Good things have to have a price because that is just the way things are.

On the way to school he passed a horse corral with two young horses and a burro together. He started bringing sugar cubes and small carrots to feed to them and longed to be able to ride on them. He liked their smell and the feel of their soft skin and the breath from their nostrils on his neck and cheeks. They would trot up to him, grab the treat, then bolt off to run around and kick up dust. Oh how Ritchie wished he could ride them and be a cowboy.

One Saturday he gobbled up his oatmeal and took off to the horse corral at a canter, slapping his hip in unison with his plopping feet to sound like a horse. He went through the fence rails and first approached the docile little burro. With his heart beating furiously, he pulled himself aboard. The burro just stood there. Ritchie urged him on with his bony knees and heels, but to no avail. Finally, the burro just got bored with it all and began to walk about slowly. Not much fun. Not very exciting. The boy slid off and stared at the burro for a minute, then began eyeing the horses. They stood side-by-side watching him too. He calculated they were not close enough to the fence to climb up the fence and get on but — but there was a tree. A tree with a good-sized branch right at the proper level. Ideal. Ritchie climbed the tree and made his way out on the branch, jockeyed around until his legs dangled off the side and waited and waited until at last the one with the all white face miraculously got himself in the right position, mindlessly chomping a bit of grass. *Now is my chance*, he thought. The would-be cowboy spread his legs just so, dropped down on the back of the unwary animal, grabbed the mane, and hung on for dear life. The horse took off at a dead run, skipping along on his flying feet until he came to the fence where he made a very agile, quick, right-angle turn. The buckaroo was launched over the rail where he hit hands and face first on the rocky ground. His wind was knocked out and it took a minute until he could yelp like a wounded animal, but then, yelp he did. His hands were all scratched up and a stone hit and nicked his forehead, so he was bleeding some. He finally shut up when he realized that there was no one around to hear anyway. He shoved his hands in his front pockets and began a slow trudge home. Disappointed, embarrassed and alone, still spitting dirt out between his teeth, he vowed to himself that he would return, but it was a while before he did.

I mention he was alone because that was the case. Brother Arne found some neighbor boys that were not too far away. Unfortunately, they were a year older than Arne himself and wanted nothing to do with his little brother. He had friends at school, but he was not allowed to have them over to his house. He simply was not allowed any such thing. Mother, with six kids at home, was not too amenable to others hanging around.

Lonesome. Ritchie was lonesome. Lonely and bored. One time he met two boys in the pasture near his home. They seemed friendly at first. Somehow they talked the city kid into peeing on an electric fence. Not a good idea, shocking. When the fun was over, they began pushing him down and tried tripping him. Ritchie ended up bawling like a calf, exclaiming he was going to tell his big brother on them and they would be sorry. They just threw dried-up horse turds at him and he ran home.

He spent his time catching frogs by the hundreds that he put in big jars with air holes punched in the lid. He wondered why sometimes they were stuck together belly to back. He would pull them apart, separate them, then watch as the one scampered over and leaped on the other again.

A boy at school that Ritchie played with on the playground at recess asked him to come home with him after school on Friday to spend two nights, go to church with them on Sunday and then his parents would take him home after church. Fine, Ritchie was happy to. He got a note to ride home with him after school on the big yellow school bus packed with kids. This would be fun. Ritchie looked around wishing that he were in on this school bus thing too. Everyone knew each other and although there was a definite pecking order, at least there was contact. They called each other names, stuck out their tongues and threw spit-wads and things. They made a lot of noise until the bus driver made them all shut up — as best he could anyway. Ritchie liked being with these after-school kids and found no trouble joining in.

There were two distinct and separate districts at Lakeland school. One included the people who lived out in the countryside on stump farms in trailers, doublewides, and humble houses with rusted car bodies, junk and chicken coops in the yard. Ritchie's own house had an old trailer that they used for a chicken coop. The roof was sagging in and the sides were covered with mold around the cracked and broken windows. Some places still had outside toilets. By contrast, the people who lived where Ritchie's friend David lived along Lake Washington and above, had very nice homes, beach property with docks and boats, and houses with nice lawns and flowers, well-dressed children and bicycles and scooters, all with an air of prosperity and contentment. Looking like today's sublime suburbia.

It went well at first. David had a rather large stuffed hobbyhorse in his basement, complete with saddle and bridle that looked very real. Ritchie had a fine time riding the stuffing out of it with his fantasy going wild as he imagined the wind on his face. They played with blocks that were designed to make a house, an electric train that went "choo-choo" all around the room, over bridges, under tunnels, through little towns and into stations it went. Ritchie stopped and started it a dozen times and delighted in tooting its whistle. They rode bikes up and down the street. Davy had a sister who was gone somewhere so Ritchie rode her bike. The girl's bike with the curved down middle like girls' bikes have made him wonder. He had banged his own stuff on the bars of his brother's bike a few times. Man, that hurts. With the girl's bike there was not that danger. The boy pledged to himself that if he ever got a bike of his own, it would be the girl kind, no matter who said what.

The boys were eventually called in to supper by Davy's mother. They put the bikes away in the garage and trudged up the stairs to the kitchen. Davy's mother wore a blue dress and a white apron with flowers on it that were about the same color blue as her dress. Her face broke into a wide, friendly smile as she ordered the "men" to go wash their hands. When they returned to the dining room off the kitchen, David's father was standing there waiting at one end of the table. He was kind of fat with a big red face and a head that was going bald from the front, back. He looked friendly enough, but some-what preoccupied or something.

"Joe, this is Ritchie. What is your last name?"

"Pelton," the boy replied.

"Joe, this is Ritchie Pelton, Davy's little school friend."

Father stuck his hand out to shake. Ritchie had never shook hands in his life, but somehow he knew not to just limp, so he squeezed — with all his might, as he pumped the hand up and down, then let go. Joe looked startled for a moment, then grinned widely.

"Howdy-do Ritchey Pelton, Joe Browne here."

"Howdy-do Mr. Browne," came back the flus-tered kid.

"Let's eat," said Joe Browne, and everyone found their seat, leaving the obvious one for Ritchie.

Ritchie sat, embarrassed about he knew not what, then pulled his napkin in his lap when he saw the others do it. Then mother, father, David folded their hands in a prayerful pose, bowed their heads:

"Come Lord Jesus, be our guest so this food will all be blessed. Amen," said together in singsong fashion.

What a nice dinner — roast beef, mashed pota-toes, gravy, string beans and little brown buns still fresh from the oven, with celery, pickles and black olives for salad.

Ritchie was hungry and his self-consciousness disappeared as he helped himself to the food in front of him and more when it was passed around. Ritchie noticed that David's plate was filled by his father. Odd, he thought.

Ritchie was feeling full and satisfied when he looked across the table at David. He had a blank look on his unhappy face and there were tears in his eyes just starting to dribble down his cheeks.

What on earth was wrong?

"You eat everything on your plate boy!" Davy's father hissed at him under his breath. "You are going to clean up your plate if you have to sit here all night — you hear me!"

With that, David began sniffing for real and more silent tears cut loose. He poked some mashed potatoes and gravy in his yap looking like it would gag him, swallowed quickly and kept it up in that fashion until they were gone. His mother, not unsympathetically, reached over his shoulder and cut his meat into morsels. He poked one in at a time until they were gone. That left a pile of string beans. David just stared at them. Ritchie just stared period. He clutched his glass of milk to his lips and just sipped to make it last for something to do with himself in the tense surroundings.

"I don't like string beans," the crestfallen boy muttered quietly.

"You just eat half of them," his mother said politely.

"He'll eat every goddamned one," his father said tensely, almost shouting. "Clean up your plate!"

For David it was hopeless. He skewed half at a time on his fork, like a pitchfork lifting hay and in two loads had them all in his mouth at the same time. His cheeks bulged and his eyes watered. He chewed a few times, then swallowed with an audible gasp, washed down with a slug of milk, some of which came out his nose. Anyhow, down it went. No one looked very satisfied with things, but Mother Browne made an effort to be jovial, clearing the table with a hum.

Ritchie was confused. Confused by two or three things. Why didn't Davy eat all the good food? It certainly was fine. At his house there were six kids, everyone took what they could of what they wanted or lost out. If someone didn't like string beans, someone else did. Why have to eat something you don't like? Ritchie was rather glad he liked everything. Everything except liver, anyway.

Why was David's father mean to him? Was he mad at him for something? Why the contest at the dinner table that was supposed to be a happy place and upset everyone? That was a war and Ritchie really didn't know who had won or who had won what.

Looked like a tie to me, Ritchie thought to himself.

The boys went to David's room where there were two bunk beds with a bed stand between them and David's own radio. Gall, what a lucky guy. They listened to the Friday night programs that all the boys listen to — "The Shadow" with Lamont Cranston who could cloud men's minds to make himself invisible, "The Lone Ranger" who redefined the William Tell Overture, and "I Have a Mystery," and on Saturday night, Jack Benny and Red Skelton.

After awhile listening (and watching) the radio when David's mother poked her head in:

"Get your pajamas on and come down for a piece of cake," she said merrily.

Pajamas? His sister wore pajamas. He slept raw.

David pulled on his pajamas and Ritchie followed him into the kitchen where two dishes with nice pieces of chocolate cake sat on the table.

David's mother looked at them.

"Did you forget pajamas Ritchie?"

"No, nope, I don't use them, because I don't even have any."

"Oh my, tsk, tsk," she went quietly. "Well, eat your cake and we will see what we can do."

After they had finished their cake (Davy had no trouble with that), they went back to his room.

"You boys take a shower bath now," Mother said, "I will find Ritchie some pajamas."

Well, at Ritchie's house he didn't have a shower bath, just a bathtub that he used once or twice a week. It was a real treat for him to stand under the cascading sprinkler with warm water in an endless supply drenching his hair and covering his body. It was fun for him and he was smiling again for the first time since the tense dinner.

Not only did Davy's mother find him a pair of pajamas, she gathered up all of his clothes, socks, underpants and all to take them to the washing machine. She had emptied out the contents of his pockets and left them neatly on the bedside dresser — two marbles, a large rubber band, twenty-five cents in change, a one dollar bill, a pretty little red rock, and a silver bottle cap with the writing worn off from exposure to the elements. The pajamas were laid out on the bed, and since Davy was gone already, he supposed rightly they were for him.

Davy was a big boy. Ritchie was not. The PJs hung on him and he felt like a clown. He stood by the bed looking at himself in the mirror wondering if all rich kids had to wear clothes to sleep in.

Davy's mother came bustling back into the room with Davy right behind.

"Don't you look nice?"

No, he thought.

"All clean and shiny. Dry your hair and come into the kitchen for some applesauce."

More food?

Davy was making automobile sounds pushing a toy truck with his foot as Ritchie vigorously rubbed his mop of hair with the towel. He didn't have a comb, so he ran his fingers through his hair to create some semblance of order, and then followed Davy to the kitchen where little bowls of applesauce were set out with gingersnaps warm from the oven.

The eating project went well indeed. Davy ate six gingersnaps and inhaled applesauce with a grin this time and was rewarded with another scoop of applesauce and little box of raisins.

Ritchie didn't like gingersnaps but managed to eat one to be polite. The applesauce was good however, and he enjoyed slurping it out of his spoon. Davy made a pig noise at him, so he quit that.

Going to bed with clothes on was new.

I just sleep raw, he thought, *Like an Indian.*

The legs wadded up over his knees and the crotch part pinched his little nuts so he had to pull it loose all the time. The shirt came up under his arms and the buttons felt hard to lie on.

When he woke in the morning his PJs were off. He would have slept better than he actually did, but Davy snored like a moose trapped in the mud.

"Fat people snore," he thought, remembering his uncle Oscar sleeping on the couch one night while visiting.

His clean clothes appeared on his bed while he was in the bathroom taking his morning piss.

"Always wash your hands after going to the bathroom," the mother chirped through the door at him.

"Uh-huh" Ritchie answered without commitment.

He crawled into his clothes still warm from the dryer. They smelled good and seemed softer than they did at home where they were dried on the clothesline.

"Nice."

The day went good. They played down by the lake, skipping rocks at the ducks and wading up to their knees in cold Lake Washington with the mud squishing between their toes. They had a good time. Ritchie was aware that it was good to have someone to play with.

The little public beach area was next to a house built right on the shore with a dock next to it. A boy their own age came out his door and, ignoring them completely, went over and climbed into a nice little rowboat untied himself and began to row around in jig-jags and big circles. He was a very skillful rower and it was apparent that he was showing off his skill, still ignoring the boys completely.

"That's Gary," Davy said. "Nobody likes him. He goes to a private Catholic school. He is a big snob."

Ritchie saw the boy looking curiously at them every now and then with a serious look on his face that didn't seem fitting. Didn't the look seem, well, longing for something?

Snobs may just be boys who want to play but don't know how to join in, he mused to himself. *Other kids should invite them or something.*

He started to say something but stopped when Davy threw a mud ball at him, which demanded reprisal.

Gary tied up his rowboat again and went back into his house without looking back.

Odd. Ritchie had a momentary tug of sympathy for him. *I wish I had talked to him,* he thought.

After a lunch of hot soup and grilled cheese, washed down with cold milk, Davy's mother took them in her station wagon and dropped them off at the show in Lake City where the Saturday matinee was showing a Hopalong Cassidy movie as well as a Bugs Bunny cartoon and a Bud Abbott and Lou Costello movie about a haunted house. Double features and a cartoon. What will happen to them? While they were waiting in line to get their tickets (Davy paid for both of them because his mother told him to even though Ritchie had his own dollar), the boy Gary showed up behind them in line. Without thinking at all, Ritchie turned to him.

"I saw you rowing your boat," he said. "You really are good at it."

Gary didn't even answer.

The look on his face was a distrustful sneer.

Asshole, Ritchie thought as he followed Davy into the show.

After the show Davy's mother picked them up and drove to a store that had a lunch counter. What a treat. They had hamburgers, French fries and malts for dinner. They laughed as they retold the Abbott and Costello show with appropriate sound effects. Davy's mother looked amused as well. It was nice.

"Where is Dad?" Davy asked with more concerned that seemed warranted.

"He won't be home until later," is all she said.

Davy got quiet and the air grew thick.

Father wasn't there in the morning to take them all to church either. This time Davy didn't ask where he was but seemed resigned to something. Ritchie's father was gone a lot because he worked in a logging camp in Northbend. Sometimes he didn't get home even for the weekends. Everyone was glad to see him when he did come home, but no one in his house seemed to miss him when he wasn't there.

Fathers sometimes don't come home. They are different than mothers, who have to be there, Ritchie thought.

The night went better. Ritchie just took off his silly PJs and slept in his underpants (which had been washed and dried again), so he slept well. He dreamed he was in a rowboat trying to row up a stream, but he just couldn't get the oars coordinated in any kind of rhythm. He awoke once in the middle of the night aware that he wanted to go home, but soon fell back asleep to the rhythmic honk of Davy's snoring.

The church was something else again for him. Davy's mother was dressed up in a pretty blue dress with a collar to her chin and ruffles on her sleeves. She smelled of lavender and left an air behind her when she left the room. Ritchie thought she was pretty. She wore a smile that wasn't quite all there, but was very cheerful.

Davy was dressed in corduroy pants and a white shirt. Ritchie had only the clothes he had brought; as a matter of fact, he had no better ones anyway. Davy's mother put a red sweater on him that was too big, but helped a lot, and off they went.

They pulled up in front of the small church that looked like it had been built from an old school-house, the plan being that they would take him home after. Frankly, he could hardly wait. He wanted to go home.

From inside the church, music was bellowing and blasting out trumpets and drums and a clanging piano. He could hear people muttering and occasionally shouting:

"Amen."

"Praise the Lord!"

"Hallelujah!"

When he walked in people had their arms waving in the air, singing in a chanting way:

"He is moving, He is moving" over and over.

Ritchie was scared to death and almost wet his pants in awestruck fear. In his church, Christian Science, things were quiet, dignified, with an atmosphere of pleasant control. He had never seen people acting like this. He would have jumped out the window if he could to get away. People hugged each other, wept, and some fell first on their knees, then onto the floor with shrieks and moans of all kinds.

Presently, the preacher began a sermon that started out fairly quietly, but ended in gyrations and pleading, supplications for poor unforgiven sinners. Ritchie was sure he was one of those. Whatever they were. All he wanted to do was get out of there. He learned that bad, bad things happened to good people and that was bad enough!

When the action stopped with loud singing, and hand clapping and a few more hallelujahs and amen's, he beat it out the door. Davy's mother, who had been wide-eyed as the rest, looked normal again with her usual smile and calm manner.

No one mentioned the service at all. (Ritchie was glad; he didn't know what to say.) It was like nothing happened in there.

They climbed in the car and Davy's mother got a few directions to take Ritchie home. It was an odd, quiet ride. Davy and Ritchie hardly looked toward each other, and said nothing.

The driveway that led to Ritchie's house was about a quarter of a mile long, a dirt and gravel road leading through a swampy area. Ritchie had her stop on the main road, telling her that the driveway road was really not passable because of mud and ruts. Really, he just didn't want them to see his house with junk lying around and an old, decrepit travel trailer with a saggy roof that was used as a chicken house. The house needed paint and the additions that had been tacked onto it were unfinished and crudely done. He did not want them to see it. Their house and all around them were very nice, well kept and presentable.

Davy's mother got out of the car, opened the trunk and fetched out a large shopping bag.

"Here, Ritchie," she smiled, "These are for you"

She seemed quite pleased. Ritchie was not. Inside were clothes faded from wear and wash. On top, a pair of pajamas with little bears on them. Horrors. Ritchie mumbled a "thank you for everything" and took off down the driveway at a fast walk. He did not look back. After he heard their car pull away, he came to a fir stump left over from logging in yesteryear. The center was all rotted out leaving a cavity. Ritchie pushed the bag way down until it about went out of sight.

He then turned and ran the rest of the way home with a smile and a light heart, which had not been his for hours.

******

Ritchie and Davy played together at school about every day, but Ritchie refused any more invitations to Davy's house and he was not about to ask him to his.

About a month later, Ritchie noticed that Davy had become quiet and sullen. He wasn't much fun to be around and was biting his fingernails to the quick. Finally, Ritchie asked, "What's the matter with you?"

Davy started bawling on the playground, rubbing his eyes with his pudgy, curled up fists.

"My dad is gone for good," he bawled. "My mom and dad are getting a divorce."

"Oh," said Ritchie. He hardly knew what that was, but he felt his friends pain and insecurity.

"My mom and me are going to move to Spokane."

With that he sat down on the ground and ground his fists into his eyes even more.

Ritchie patted him on the back halfheartedly without saying anything, then walked back into the school building because the bell was ringing.

Davy didn't come in at all and in a little while his mother showed up in class, gathered his things and with the briefest of smiles at Ritchie, left with a shopping bag of books, pencils and crayons and went out the classroom door without closing it. Ritchie noticed that the shopping bag was the same as the one all covered with various stars that he had deposited in the stump. Sadness filled the room, but Ritchie knew that only he and the teacher really knew why.

It was a bad time after that. Ritchie missed the fat-faced boy he spent his recesses with. At home there was no one to play with at all. Big brother Arne was only one and a half years older and was gone with his friends who were a year older than him and wanted nothing to do with Ritchie tagging along.

Ritchie was lonely. Money was scarce at home. His father worked in Northbend and often came home only one weekend a month. He was surly, and even more so after drinking beer. His mother and father fought and yelled at each other a lot. When his father left again, his mother was pouty, distracted, irritable and angry, and showed no affection at all. His mother was devout in the Christian Science religion, and spent hours mumbling over her books. She raised a terrible fist when disturbed and at other times went into a screaming fit for no apparent reason, then proceeded not to say a word for days. Grandma and sister looked after him. Ritchie knew to stay away from his mother altogether at times like that. If divorce ever happened in his house, he wished he could go with his father.

In the spring again it was pleasant walking three miles to school. One day a girl about his age (now 11, soon to be 12) was walking with him. It wasn't long before Ritchie was talking with the friendly miss.

"My name is Dora Mae," the girl said with a smile that lit up her face like sunbeams on a pond. The dimples on her cheeks deepened themselves with her smile, instantly becoming part of her personality. Her dress was faded light blue with a funny collar that made it look old-fashioned. Her not-quite-together blond hair was down to her shoulders without a trace of curl, while cut across her forehead were perfect bangs, like they had been cut with a ruler.

To Ritchie's surprise, she thrust out her arm to shake hands. Ritchie took her hand and cranked a little shake, although he was embarrassed to distraction.

"I am Ritchie. I am sort of new here too — nine months. What grade are you in? Who is your teacher?" he asked.

"Miss Walker," she answered. "Where are you?"

"Same room as you, fifth grade. There is only one fifth grade."

"I know where you live. You live down the long driveway on 26th. I saw you once walking down there."

"Uh-huh."

"You know the big patch of woods on the other side of 26th? Right through there to 25th is where we live." She chuckled when she talked. "We are neighbors."

"Yeah, neighbors a half a mile apart," Ritchie came back with a grin.

"We have two cows and a calf. My dad is a policeman, a sheriff. He is going to get me a horse this weekend. Do you like horses?"

Ritchie unconsciously rubbed the old wound on this forehead.

"Yes I do. I wish I had one."

They met each day and walked to school together. Ritchie threw rocks at birds and kicked a can all the way to school one day. Dora walked along looking amused at him because she knew he was self-conscious and was trying to be a male for her. Often the subtle smile on her face made her look like she had a sweet secret. She knew the names of several birds and called out their name when she saw one.

"My mother is a birdwatcher," she proudly reported.

"We don't have school Friday," Dora said one day. "Do you want to come over to my house?"

"Okay," Ritchie replied without hesitation.

They made plans and Ritchie found the way through the woods to her house by a well-worn cow trail. He was anxious for Friday to come, and when it did he was up early and on his way by nine o'clock. He walked slowly, knowing it was early. He did not want to seem too eager, but he was. He stopped by the edge of the woods and looked at her house. It was white, freshly painted, with shutters painted a light gray. The small yard had a white picket fence around it with a gate on a spring. The walk to the front door was gravel, punctuated by flat stepping stones laid out in alternate rows. Small flowers, or plants anyway, were struggling through the ground on each side of the path. A sheriff's patrol car was parked in the driveway.

With some hesitation the boy walked up to the door, opened the screen and tapped on the door. Not really much of a knock.

Rather quickly the door swung open and a lady stood looking down at him. Her smile welcomed him with a flash of white teeth and freshly painted lips. Ritchie noticed immediately that her round cheeks contained dimples as well.

"Is Dora home?" Ritchie stammered.

"Sure is, young man. Are you Ritchie?"

"Yes, ma'am."

"Dora Mae," she called out over her shoulder. "Your gentleman caller is here."

The woman giggled pleasantly and ushered him in, leaving the door open but the screen closed.

Dora skittled into the room followed by a stringy little girl, about five, with bony knees and elbows everywhere, wearing a look both curious and welcoming.

"Hi there. My dad's asleep. This is my sister, Elizabeth Mae. We call her Liz because she looks like a lizard."

"Dora Mae! That's not nice!" Mother said sternly.

Dora reached over quickly and hugged Liz's shoulder. There was a slight resemblance to a lizard.

"Come on, let me show you my horse." She pulled on the boy's sleeve a second, then beat it out the door with Liz following uninvited behind. Ritchie hurried to keep up on the way to a barn and surrounding corral behind the house. There stood a small black horse with a Roman nose and hoofs that were too large, a shaggy thick mane and a tail that touched the ground. A typical stunted Mustang.

"He looks wild, but he is really tame and friendly. He was trained and broke, then turned loose for a year. My dad is having a cowboy come over and ride him a few times to be sure he is safe for me. He will look better with this hooves trimmed too."

She let out a sucking-hissing sound with her pursed lips as she held out a small apple. The pony walked over slowly like he was bored with it all, took the apple with his lips and chewed the whole thing at once, producing a frothy juice that dripped on the ground.

"What's his name?" Ritchie asked.

"I haven't named him yet. What do you think?"

"Is he a boy or a girl?" Ritchie asked.

"Neither one, dummy. Humans are boys and girls. Animals are males and females. He is a male, but has had his balls cut off, so he is called a gelding."

She said this quite matter-of-factly without a hint of embarrassment.

"Oh," said Ritchie trying to act wise. He looked at the horse with deep aching envy tugging at his insides. When they, Ritchie's family, had moved up from Seattle, his mother told him maybe they would have a horse. He knew after awhile that wasn't about to happen. Still, the want was there along with a kernel of hope he held inside.

Dora had a little playhouse under a big tree in her backyard. It was filled with all kinds of junk: old magazines, newspapers, cracked and scratched 45 records, rags and unidentifiable pieces of wire and metal things, as well as derelict furniture, broken chairs, rotten smelling pillows, and cracked lamp-shades.

"Daddy says if we clean it out nice, it is ours. Will you help us?"

"Sure," said Ritchie.

Dora ran into the house and pretty soon a pick-up truck came backing up to the playhouse from around the house. Mom was driving and Dora ran alongside.

"Don't hurt yourselves, kids," she said as she returned to the house. Ritchie lowered the tailgate on the old Plymouth pick-up and they began piling things in. Some things, like a piece of old bedsprings, required two people to handle, Dora on one side and Ritchie on the other. Little Liz always grabbed a hold and groaned loudest of all. Ritchie was aware of a certain feeling of satisfaction that he and Dora were working together like this. It felt fine. He found himself patronizing Liz like an older brother — or parent. That made "dimples" smile a lot. He found himself looking forward to having it cleaned all out so he could move in there.

At noontime, Dora's mother called out, "Come in for lunch." She shuttled the kids into the bathroom. "You are all grimy, dirty little gypsies. Wash your hands and face with soap!" After they sat down at the table that was both the kitchen and dining room table, Ritchie was aware that he felt very comfortable. Liz scampered around so she was sitting next to Ritchie, her knobby little knees banging his as she squirmed into her seat. An adjoining door opened and Dora's father emerged from the bedroom. He was wiping his eyes and rubbing his chin. He soon smiled at everyone, then came over to sit down. He was wearing pajamas! My God, he was wearing pajamas! Ritchie was at a loss as to what to think of that. He thought kids wore pajamas. *I'll be jiggered,* thought Ritchie.

"This is Ritchie, Paul, Dora's friend."

"And Liz's friend," Liz interrupted.

"Yes, and Liz's friend too," Mom said with a wink at Ritchie. "He is our neighbor and he goes to school with Dora."

"I didn't think we had any neighbors," Paul said. "Where do you live?"

"On the other side of 26th."

"Where the long driveway is?"

"Yes."

"Well, Mr. Ritchie, what are your intentions with my daughter?"

"Paul!"

"Dad!"

Daddy Paul shrugged his shoulders without further comment.

"I am hungry," he said. "Pass the biscuits to this poor, damn cop." He sniffed the large, steaming bowl in front of him.

"Aw, rabbit stew!"

"Paul, that's chicken stew!"

"Oh," he said, "I was hopin' it was bunny."

Everyone laughed, including Ritchie and Liz.

After lunch, Daddy Paul stood up and scratching his belly, and "I'll get dressed and help you guys clean out the playhouse. Needs painting," he mumbled as he went back to his bedroom.

Ritchie picked up his dishes as was his custom at home and brought them to the sink. "I'll wash and you girls can dry because you know where to put things."

"Well I'll be," the mother mumbled under her breath. The girls looked funny too, but grabbed dish towels, exchanging glances with their mother.

In the next few weeks the playhouse was cleaned out and painted the same color as the house. Sometimes after school and always on Saturday, Ritchie was there spending time with the girls. It was a nice game of playing house. Ritchie the daddy, Dora the mama, and Liz their little make-believe daughter. Dora started calling him "Darling" and "Honey," and when play was done, she kissed him on the cheek and sent him "off to work." Liz demanded a kiss from Ritchie and received it on the top of her head as any good daddy would.

Spring became summer and when school was out, they played almost everyday at various things, but usually in the same roles.

The cowboy had "taken the buck" out of the ugly little horse and he became a wonderful pony. There was no saddle and they got very good at grabbing the mane and swinging up. Dora and Ritchie became more adept as time went on and soon were galloping all over in the cow pasture and up an down the dusty roads. One day they rode to where Ritchie had launched himself from the tree onto the surprised horse. The boy showed her the scar on his forehead and they laughed together.

To begin with Dora rode in front with Ritchie holding on around her waist, but after awhile when they rode double, Ritchie insisted on being in front because "that's where the man should be." Poor Liz was left behind waving at them from the barn with a blank smile. Once when Dora's father Paul was home, he came running out.

"Hold up," he said. He lifted Liz up and sat her between them with a laugh. Everyone laughed as they trotted off across the pasture. It was impossible to hang on because they all bounced, really bounced at a little different time until all three were spilled on the ground in a tangle of arms and legs with oops and awes. The horse stepped away, looked back in utter disgust, and took off at a dead run back to his home in the barn. It was funny and fun.

Ritchie found himself thinking about Dora and her family a lot and wished that he lived there. Love was a little scarce in his house with his father gone most of the time, brothers and sisters with their lives and his mother with craziness, silent sullenness, and wild temper tantrums that made him afraid of her most of the time. So, he spent as much time as he could with Dora, playing daddy sometimes and cowboy at others.

A fair sized creek passed through a big pasture with an orchard at one end. It was a great place to go fishing. Great all the more because the lady who lived there on the other side of the creek forbid anyone trespassing, let alone fishing in the creek. If she saw them, she would come out threatening and yelling, waving her broom in the air at them. The kids got smart and started waiting for the old Buick sedan to pull out of her yard before they made their way down the hill from the orchard to the creek. They had fishing poles cut from willow branches with a length of line on the end, six-inch leaders of nylon, and worm hooks with a glob of wiggling worms on them. They hooked lots fish, but only caught a few that they kept in a plastic bread sack to take home. Sometimes Dora's mother or father would flavor them up and cook them, but lots of times they just disappeared somehow in the kitchen under the sink.

One bright day in August, Dora and Ritchie sneaked themselves down to the creek and managed to lose their hooks on snags. They were done fishing because that's the only hooks they had. Disappointed, they trudged up the hill in the sun and sat down on the grass under an old half-worn out apple tree.

"Listen, Ritchie," Dora said quietly, "You can hear lots of things if you listen. Close your eyes."

Ritchie closed his eyes and listened intensely. He heard grasshoppers rubbing their legs together, a tree frog crack a little song, young birds fanning the air with their new-found wings. He even heard the wings of a butterfly that swam in the air near his ear. Down below, the creek laughed at the day as it splashed over rocks making swirls of foam that sparkled with the sun behind them. Birds chirped and whistled to each other. Ritchie and Dora kept their eyes closed for a long time, saying nothing at all, just listening together with the sun hot on their cheeks. Ritchie reached over slowly and took her hand in his. She responded with a contented sight as she squeezed his fingers lightly. Then the lad leaned over and tried to kiss her on the mouth. She giggled and turned away from his bungling effort

"Silly," she laughed, and Ritchie laughed too because he didn't know what else to do, embarrassed and disappointed in a way.

In a moment Dora looked over at him with a quizzical smile.

"Ritchie, look up there." She pointed to the top of the old tree. Most of the apples were gone but there remained a big bright red one on a limb by itself. "If you get me that apple, I'll kiss with you," she said seriously.

Ritchie did not reply, but slipped off his shoes, grabbed hold of a low limb and began pulling himself up branch by branch, clinging with his toes as well as his hands.

"Be careful," she admonished.

Ritchie didn't answer, making his way to the limb with the prize apple. He wrapped himself around the limb and crawled out slowly until he was able to reach it. As he did so, the old limb let out a creak of protest, bent unnaturally and split partway through under him. He managed to grab the fruit with a large piece of stem and make his way back holding the apple by the stem in his mouth. It was hard to hold on because he couldn't help smiling. On the ground he presented the prize to her. It was all red on one side from exposure to the sun and nicely speckled on the other side. It was still warm from the sun. When she bit into the reddest part, juice flowed out in abundance. She laughed as she wiped off her chin and cheeks with the back of her little hand.

"There," she said as she held it out. He chomped himself a huge bite and made a big show of wiping the juice away. Together they finished the fruit until only the core remained held delicately in Dora's fingers. She handed it to Ritchie who threw it as hard as he could down the hill.

They stood there for a moment, then Dora put both hands around the apprehensive boy's neck, pulled him gently to her, and kissed his ready lips, puckered for the occasion. A soft smack was made as she pulled back.

"Thanks for the apple."

"Thanks for the kiss."

Ritchie knew something very subtle had changed between them. It made him anxious in a way, but he didn't really mind.

The Friday evening show became an event that was rarely missed. Ritchie would hike over to Dora's house in the early evening and either Dora's mother or father would drive them to the theater at Lake City. Dora's little sister usually came along too. At first, Ritchie would be hesitant to hold her hand with Liz there, but after awhile it didn't seem to matter, so he would clutch her hand and hold it through most of the movie, usually between them, but on this occasion in his lap. Ritchie was chewing away on a piece of worn out gum, trying to keep his mixed up mind of — things — and on the show.

"Give me a piece of gum."

"I haven't got any more. This was my only piece."

"Yes you do. I feel a package in you pocket."

With this, she released his hand and quickly pushed her hand down into his front pocket as he stiffened and wiggled. She grabbed at the object of her search and found that it was outside the pocket itself and attached to him.

She let go immediately but was slow taking her hand out of his pocket, trying not to make a fuss. The girl giggled and shook and held her hand over her mouth to soften her giggle.

Poor Ritchie simply slumped down in his seat and tried to act nonchalant as he could. He knew his face was so red that his ears probably glowed in the dark.

The fall of the year passed into wet winter. It got dark earlier so Ritchie found himself almost running through the pasture, down the trail through the woods and down his long driveway through the swamp. He was aware he was kind of afraid in the dark. Afraid of what? He didn't know. Not the dark itself, but the idea that he could not see or know what was ahead. He found himself reasoning to himself, talking out loud in a soft voice.

What am I afraid of? Am I just a big sissy or something? There are no wild animals that are going to jump out and get me. There ain't no bogyman. That is kids' stuff. Silly. Anytime a person closes their eyes, it is dark. I wonder if it is all dark when you are dead? (The thought gave him no comfort, let alone courage.) He forced himself to walk slowly, trudging along peering into the trees and bushes as he went.

I am walking home! he said to himself with conviction. *There is nothing to be scared of anyhow.* He had heard somewhere once or twice that dead people, ghosts or spirits roamed around at night. Even if they did, why would they want to hurt anyone? Maybe just scare kids for the fun of it. The only one he knew that was dead was grandma. *She sure wouldn't want to harm me or even scare me.* He felt a little better — very little.

Forcing himself to walk at a slow pace, he whistled into the night, not making any tunes at all. He wondered about dying once more and he remembered that he was taught in Sunday School not to be afraid. *Jesus will come and pick you up and take you to a heaven place up in the sky somewhere because Jesus loves us and doesn't want us to be afraid and God is…*

Just then a lone duck took off from the swamp next to the driveway.

Ritchie ran the rest of the way home as fast he could.

The days were pretty much the same. Ritchie would find himself at Dora's house, usually right after lunch. They would climb on the ugly little horse and run his legs off until he didn't want to run anymore, so would jog along nicely. He always seemed to be grateful when he was turned back into the corral. He would roll over with grunts and moans, covering himself with dust and dirt that would eventually dry to a fine powder that was brushed off before the next ride. Dora would beam at him and say good-bye as they went to the playhouse. Liz would usually come, too. Dora would be like the mother while Ritchie the father and Liz like their offspring. It wasn't like little children playing house. In fact, it is hard to explain exactly how the game started and continued. Sometimes they would even pretend that they were having little marital squabbles ending with Ritchie getting a kiss on the cheek to make up. They both knew it was kind of silly and childish, but somehow neither wanted to stop the game. Ritchie liked swaggering around with his thumb in his belt while Dora fussed over him and Liz looked on approvingly.

So that's how it went. Things were nice for them. They were happy, and better, they knew it.

One early Saturday, Ritchie came over. He brought two freshly cut willow fishing poles with string, leaders and hooks attached. A can of worms he held in his hand.

Dora came out her door when she saw the boy approach. She looked pale tired in the eyes.

"I don't feel good, honey," she said. She usually only called him honey when they were playing family. "I just want to go lay down. My throat is really sore."

"That's all right, Dora, I'll come back tomorrow maybe."

"Okay," she said as she turned to return to the house. She stopped, paused for a moment, then came up to Ritchie and kissed him on the mouth. He felt her usually soft lips on his and was aware that they were dry and hot.

Ritchie went home. He didn't feel like going fishing anymore.

It was a few days later, with Dora absent from school awhile, that a man came to their door with a sheriff in uniform tagging along behind. He held signs that said "Quarantine, No Passage" with thick red print on the bottom that said diphtheria. A small paragraph of fine lettering spelled out legislation.

Ritchie's mother threw open the door angrily.

"What do you want here?" she demanded.

The man with a necktie was courteous.

"Ma'am," he said with only a hint of apology, "This place is under quarantine now. It is the law. Your son is friends with the folks on the other side of the pasture and woods there." He pointed across the road. "The Ross family. Your son Richard is exposed to diphtheria. You are not to leave your house and no one can come here for two weeks. This is serious legal business," he added with emphasis, gesturing toward the policeman.

"Well, we don't believe in sickness in this house." She was almost screeching. "We are Christian Scientist and you just go away." She grabbed the paper out of his hand, threw it down and was attempting to slam the door when the policeman stepped up and held it back with his foot.

"Hey lady, we don't want any trouble. This is bad enough as it is, for Christ's sake. You are going to be posted and obey the quarantine or go to jail." He talked loudly, firmly, but not unkindly.

Ritchie's mother just stood there with her eyes bulging in anger while I listened from inside the porch.

"Is Dora all right?" Ritchie squeaked.

The man with the tie kneeled down on one knee with a cloud over his face.

"Are you Richard?" he asked.

"Uh-huh," Ritchie replied.

"Are you sick, son? Do you have a sore throat?"

"He is not sick," his mother said with a vitriolic tone.

"Let him answer, damn it!" the Sheriff said with unmistakable authority.

"No, I am not sick. How's Dora and Liz?"

The man rose again. He seemed to choke on his words.

"Elizabeth is in the hospital. She is awfully sick." Then with a little hesitation and profound kindness, "Dora died."

It was like he was numb all over. Like he had been struck by electricity and after the shock goes away, numbness, uncomfortable numbness remains.

I guess if he had cried then, if he could have cared then, rather than just feeling a frightful aching in his chest that immobilized him and made him stare off blankly; things would have been different. I don't mean better, you see. In fact, no better at all. Just different.

The man left the signs nailed to the door and to the trees and left with just a glance back.

Ritchie crawled away and folded up in a heap on the dusty, smelly couch. It is hard to know what went through his mind. Every thought seemed senseless to him. There was not a thought of any kind from his own mind that could give him any solace, but he yearned for it, to be somehow comforted.

I guess it should be told that Ritchie's mother was crazy. Nuts. A schizophrenia that came and went from angry outbursts over nothing to periods of solemn silence. From wicked spankings with wooden spoons to silent blubbering. It is no wonder his father didn't want to stay home anyhow. At this time she had brought herself together to simply leave the boy alone in his mists.

No one insisted that he eat or do anything. For two days he lay around with his mind locked into racing, sad, disquieting and frightening thoughts. *I guess I am next,* he thought. *I am scared, but I don't care either.*

Late one after noon just a few days later, Ritchie found himself walking slowly up the long driveway, through the cow pasture, then the woods, past the corral and up to the door. It was exactly like he was in dream, a stunted, uncomfortable state of separation from everything around him. He felt like something had to give way inside him, but he just didn't know what or how.

He knocked softly on the door. He was aware of soft rustling noises inside. Then the door opened and Mae was standing there looking at him with sad and hollow eyes.

"I want Dora," his voice came out like a high-pitched squeak he hardly recognized as his own.

Her hand shot up to her mouth as she stifled a cry and a sob. She reached down, lugged him inside holding him in an embrace. She sat down in the big overstuffed chair there and pulled the now sobbing boy onto her lap. His face floated down between her soft breasts as he snuggled there wetting the whole front of her blouse with the uncontrollable tears that fell like raindrops off the leaves. Her chin was in his hair, then her lips on his cheeks as her body shook gently to and fro. She rocked him and rocked him into the long shadows of evening.

It was dark when the headlights of the car lit up the windows, and when the engine stopped, footsteps came up and the door opened. The light was switched on and Father Paul took in the scene with his quizzical eyes and furrowed brow.

He approached slowly than reached down gently and took the boy from her limp arms.

"The boy has got to go home now," he said as he bent over and kissed his wife's wet face. He lifted him onto his shoulders and ducked out the door with Ritchie holding onto his whiskered cheeks. Through the forest, through the cow pasture, across the road down the long driveway to his door. Paul was sweating and panting a little as he sat him down and knocked on the door. The door flew open and Ritchie's mother stood staring at them.

"Where have you been?" she demanded as she grabbed him by the arm and pushed him inside. Dora's father said absolutely nothing, turned and walked away in the direction he had come.

"You!" his mother screeched.

"Leave him alone, ma," Harold said quickly as big sister came forward pulling him to her.

"He is a good boy," Sister said.

"Huh," his mother grunted and walked away into the kitchen leaving them locked in a hug.

"I understand, little Ritchie," Sister said quietly.

Ritchie fell asleep in his bed, curled under the covers that night and dreamt. He saw her dimpled face laughing at him. He dreamt of the big red apple and the kiss on the lips that had thrilled him. He dreamt of rides on the horse and the play with Liz in the playhouse. He dreamed and he dreamed until he heard her voice in his ear.

"Don't cry, honey, I am all right. I am safe here and you can always remember me."

There wasn't a thought that he could have out of his own mind that could give him comfort, yet he was comforted. Completely comforted by a force of love itself that filled him and emptied his grief and lifted the shades from his heart and mind.

When the quarantine signs were taken off, Ritchie trudged his way back to school, into his classroom, and sat down in his seat. Only once did he look at Dora's place where already another sat fiddling with her pencils. He found he could think again and he was glad.

That day at recess he played baseball with the boys and hit a home run that surprised everyone, including Ritchie.

He didn't get sick despite the kiss from the sick girl that should have given him diphtheria too. People thought it was kind of a miracle. Perhaps it was. His mother thought it was to be expected from her religion. Perhaps it was.

So, from death, he had to learn about life. A burden for us all. Maybe best started from a young age. Who knows.

Youngblood of the Grand Rhon

Book I

I turned off the well-worn road of ancient, cracked concrete repaired with dried out tar onto a rather smooth dirt road that ran next to a group of buildings labeled Gran Rhon Center on a cracked and worn pine board road side sign. The buildings were old but well kept; a gas station, quick stop start combination that advertised a fly shop. A very old blacksmiths' shop with an open front and with no sign of recent activity. A separate veterinary office for large and small animals that had a round corral behind it, a hideously green motel with four doors and a sign that said, *Inquire at store*. I noticed another small white brick building that said, *Medical Clinic Open Tuesday and Thursday 9 til noon*. I wondered what people did if they got sick, say, Wednesday at 3.

The dirt road was actually an improvement over the concrete, but I had to slow down due to the dust. In only a quarter mile I came to a gate with a cattle guard on it. It was a big heavy gate made of a black iron with the welding still showing. There was a sign painted on a board wired to the gate that said, *Welcome. If you don't close the gate behind you we will shoot you.*

The house, the ranch house, was made of logs that looked like they came from the surrounding forest, all uniform; about a foot in diameter and looking freshly oiled. There was a large front porch painted light blue, as were the window frames. The roof was bright red corrugated metal. I had to drive by a garden, well kept and orderly, growing sweet corn, potatoes, onion, carrots, peppers, cabbage, and lettuce. Next to the lettuce were hills of beans and squash, cucumber. At any rate, it was a nice vegetable garden with a built in sprinkler system that went off just as I went by. There must have been six lilac bushes in bloom with rose bushes interspersed all around the yard proper. On each side of the house were carefully pruned fruit trees. A white horse, a brown horse and two ugly black mules that were past their prime chomped grass in a closed in pasture. As I got out of the car, I was aware of the sound of the Gran Rhon river near by as well as the sound of crows circling overhead cawing at each other. Crows always seem to be mad at each other, or the world, or both. Mr. Youngblood sat on his porch puffing on a homemade corncob pipe. Rather, *Dr.* Youngblood; he was a veterinarian. He stood up and yelled at a great big, I mean, great big dog that was sizing me up for lunch. The damn thing looked like a cross between an Airedale and a Great Dane (surprise, that is exactly what he turned out to be). When

Dr. Youngblood yelled, "Buddy," the dog looked ashamed and approached me apologetically with his tail wagging. Big dogs scare me, but I managed to pat him on the head. The dog looked grateful and licked my hand with a tongue the size of a necktie and as wet as a mop.

"Dr. Youngblood, I am Howard Singer. It looks like I bought your property here. The ranch. I am glad to meet you at last."

"Come up and sit," gestured the old man.

I looked him over as he came. I knew that Youngblood was in his nineties, but he stood straight and moved quickly. His red face was clean-shaven and the multitude of wrinkles present were not very deep. His bright blue eyes were alert and snappy. He sported a full head of hair, which was not entirely gray, but had strands of red mixed in. His clothes were clean and colorful and he wore a nice pair of shiny cordovan boots. If Youngblood was looking me over, he didn't let on — just smiled widely and invited me to sit in a nice swinging chair.

"You want a drink?"

"Sure."

"Water, pop or buttermilk?"

"Water, please. Would be nice."

"Good water here," Youngblood said when he reappeared onto the porch from inside. "Comes from a well 500 feet deep. Cold and pure. Good water."

It was good water indeed, and I downed the whole glass. "Thanks. What is it they call you?"

"Bucky or Doc or *Guapo*."

"*Guapo*?"

"That's Spanish for handsome," he chuckled, sitting down and putting his feet up.

"People call me Howie. That's a nice set of boots, *Guapo*."

"Heh heh," went the old man. "Yeah, a patient brought them up from old Mexico for me. Rather, a patient's owner. Patient was a horse. He took a whole bunch of measurements on paper, of both my feet. They fit like a perfect glove when I first put 'em on. People make a mistake when they buy boots that ain't comfortable from the get-go."

"What can you tell me about the ranch and about you?" I asked respectfully.

"What can I tell you? I can tell you everything about both if you want to listen. I am a long-winded son of a bitch and a first class storyteller. Where to begin?"

"How did an Anglo like you get an Indian name?"

"That's a long story. Kinda complicated."

He settled back in his chair and lit his pipe. It smelled like he was smoking old barn straw or something and was the bluest pipe smoke I ever saw. I was aware of something then; actually, two things. He was lonesome as hell and he wanted to tell the story of his life. I was glad. I took mental notes and wrote them down as soon as I could. I have to say, I was surprised by what I could remember. He really could spin a tale that held my attention.

"My mother showed up in Asotin when I was about six years old. She was with some galoot that wasn't her husband and nobody thought much of either one of them. He got a job in the garage working on cars. He was dirty all the time with grease tattooed into the cracks in his hands and under his fingernails. My mother called herself Brenda Bumpf. She wore flowery dresses that were too short and always had a big bow in her hair. Her lipstick was too red and seemed always to be a little smeared. She smoked cigarettes one after the other when she could. She worked as a waitress and a bar hop there at Little Nickel Bar and Grill in Asotin.

"I don't know exactly why, but the geezer she hung out with was arrested and carried off to jail in Walla Walla. It must have been bad because he was sentenced to five years. Anyhow, off he went, leaving my mother and me on our own. I don't remember my mother being mean to me or anything, but I was left alone while she was at work and to fend for myself while she got all dolled up and went to the bars at night. Sometimes she would sneak some guy in and we always ate better after that, for awhile anyway. That's when my dad, Emerson Youngblood was his name, came into the picture.

"My mother got sick with flu and pneumonia and couldn't work. In no time, we were destitute. Emerson was involved in a welfare job of some kind. I think he was just supposed to look after Indians, but he drew no barriers. So, he got involved with her plight. He brought her and me to his home, where she stayed for five years. They had some kind of agreement and actually got along well. I remember. I remember a lot of things. Emerson would go with her to her bedroom for an hour or so, then come out carrying his clothes and go into his own room. As young as I was, I knew it was odd to say the least, but they really did get along pretty well.

"Sometimes he would get mad when she went to town and came back early in the morning smelling of booze and cigarettes, still drunk. He would always let her sleep the next day as long as she wanted and that kind of smoothed things over. Sometimes she would be gone for a couple of days, to visit her family, she said. Hell, her family was in Oklahoma. She was down to Walla Walla prison to visit her damned lover.

"Let me tell you about Emerson Youngblood, can I?"

"Sure."

"Emerson Youngblood was a full blooded Nez Perce Indian from the Oregon side of the Snake. His father raised him on a ranch, along with his two brothers, after his mother died of consumption. I never knew his brothers, but he was a leader of men, a descendent of Chief Joseph, an educated man who knew the value of education and sent his boys off to high school in mission schools. He must have been one hell of a man because Emerson Youngblood was one hell of a man. One smart, kindhearted, hard-working, wise man who had respect from everyone who knew him and care from most. He taught himself to be a farrier and a blacksmith. He got books on it and slaved himself out to the good ones around. He ran the shop there on the road. It is a mystery how he got the 600 acre ranch and the river here, a real mystery. But he owned it outright. I saw the title. Something to do with Hudson Bay Company, years ago. I don't know. Never really asked.

"Grand Rhon means Grand Rendezvous. It was a meeting place for all the old mountain men and trappers, who named it. He owned the part down the river where the Gran Rhon meets the Snake mostly, but this meadow here, too. Grand Rendezvous. Anyhow it was his, I saw the survey and the deed.

"Being an Indian was serious business to him. He talked about the Nez Perce and their horses. One time the United States Army, in all their benevolent wisdom, shot 500 Appaloosa horses just to subjugate the Indians. Emerson knew the whole story of the Nez Perce war and would tell it to anyone who wanted to listen.

"Do you know about it?" he asked.

"I think so," I said. "Pretty much." He told me anyway.

"You know, if it hadn't been for the Nez Perce, Lewis and Clark and his whole bunch would have been wiped out, starved or killed. Nez Perce had good trading practices with the French and British and even helped the American immigrants on the end of the Oregon Trail. They went to this reservation quietly because old Chief Joseph knew what was coming was inevitable and he thought war would be futile.

"The land that the Nez Perce were originally given was beautiful rolling grasslands and fertile valleys that the Indians were adapting to very well. That can't last and it didn't. The whites wanted it. They coveted it and they took it. A couple of young bucks killed an American trader who was a well-known ne'er-do-well and crooked cheater. That's all that it took. So here comes the great American Cavalry. The whole damn tribe took off. Women, children, old folks, dogs, horses. They went across Lo Lo pass if you can believe it with the soldiers biting on their poor damn heels like dogs. For one thousand miles, they kept ahead of the finest cavalry in the world. Other tribes, the Blackfoot for instance, betrayed them or they would have made it to Canada. As it was, they stopped 20 miles away from the border because they thought they were across. They were surrounded by the army, who had just a grand time taking potshots at them from a distance.

"Looking Glass. Looking Glass. He was the war chief. Joseph was the peacemaker when they surrendered. Chief Joseph was not allowed to go home until he was dead. He is buried over by Walla Walla somewhere. They locked him up at the Indian reservation there at Colville, Washington.

"Anyway, I digress. Sorry. Back to Emerson. Like a lot of Nez Perce, he was big and strong. Over six foot and not a fat day in his life. He never smoked cigarettes, but it was unusual to see him without a chew of Star plug in his cheek. Unlike a lot of Indians, he didn't drink and would not allow alcohol on the place or around him. He had seen what alcohol could do to Indians and he understood that Indians just could not drink.

"I knew about alcohol firsthand. I had been forced, shall we say, to study up on it. In some people, not all I guess, alcohol is converted to a substance in the brain no different from heroine. That enzyme is responsible for the euphoria and the craving. The alcohol people take is denatured in the liver. *Metabolized* is the word.

"Some nationalities have far more enzymes than others. The ones that have little get drunk earlier and harder, and stay drunk longer, while the enzymes in the brain make them higher, more euphoric and stay drunk better. Indians have the wretched enzyme in the brain and lack the ones in the liver. They lose all around. But there's another thing: alcohol fits into the Indian society and attitudes too well. 'The hell with tomorrow. Let's have a big party!' type thing. Emerson knew these things but he had his religion, too. Hard to explain. He wouldn't go to a white man's church after leaving the mission school. He prayed a lot. All the time. Always in Indian tongue with the eyes closed for a few seconds or, rarely, a few minutes. He had no use for all the dress and sex hang-ups we live with, and although he was honest, he dearly loved to trick people with trades like horses and guns. It was like a game to him.

"Emerson did not exactly take to me right off. I was blond, blue eyed and could be a bawl baby sometimes. I was small and thin, too. The way the Indian fed me, however, I started to grow. He even bought a milk cow that I think was especially for me. One day, there was a kind of a breakthrough. I had fallen down and scraped my knees and elbows up pretty bad and fell right into a prickly pear cactus. I had just turned seven. I didn't cry.

" 'Damn dirty shit,' I yelled (just like him). I'll never forget how he looked at me. The big man began to touch me more, you know, like patting my head, shaking my shoulder, stuff like that.

"One day he said to me, 'Let's make a couple of slingshots.'

"I thought it was one swell idea. He found a couple of trees that branched just right. He cut them and I whittled them smooth. I got an old rubber inner tube that was lying around the garage, then cut strips just the right size for me to pull and stretch. He cut the tongue out of an old pair of boots and used the leather to make the poucher. When we put it all together, we had two fine slingshots. We took a handful of marbles that he had a bag of in the garage.

" 'I used to be the marble champion of the reservation,' he said with a grin that involved his whole face.

"Man, we had a great time," Youngblood continued. "We shot at squirrels, birds, rabbits, and things like fence posts and leaves on trees. I don't remember ever hitting an animal or a bird, but it was fun. We got to be friends. I followed him everywhere and started walking and acting just like him. Hell, I still do. Things like standing with the weight on one leg with the other knee bent a little and the hip slouched forward. All cowboys do that. He always stuck his thumbs in his belt when he was talking to people. I did the same. He never took off his hat unless he was going into the house. Sometimes not even then. You know, I never saw him eat with his hat on. I see cowboys, I guess they are cowboys, in restaurants eating with their hats still on. I guess a few old timers do that too but he didn't, and neither do I. He gave me one of his old hats that was way too big. He stuck it down in boiling water and let it dry in the sun to shrink it. It was made of felt. That didn't work too well so he stuffed the inside band with toilet paper. That worked a little. At least it stayed on my punkin' head. He made me a stampede strap, you know, that goes under your chin to hold it on, and I was all fixed up.

"When school started up, it was Emerson who took me and got me started there, not my ma. The first grade through the sixth was there divided into just two rooms. The schoolhouse was just across the way from the blacksmith's shop. Not there anymore. Burned down after World War II. Kids by playing with matches.

"I really liked school and, if you will pardon me, I was smart. Somehow, my being bashful as hell then was interpreted by the teacher as being polite. So, anyway, the teachers liked me and always gave me lots of extra attention and extra work to do. I think I was the only second grader to have homework. As luck would have it, the only boys in the school were older than me by a couple of years and I wasn't about to play with girls. As I think about it though, I liked to jump rope. I got real good at it too, doing 'double dip.' So anyway, I would cross the street to the blacksmith's shop and take my lunch with Emerson. Eventually, thanks be to God, it was Dad. Before that, Emerson," the old man added respectfully.

"How did you get started calling him Dad?" I asked.

The old man leaned back and smiled as he tamped out his pipe.

"I'll get to that," he said with a wink. "After school, I would watch that big Injun pound iron. He would have me pump the bellows for him; sometimes he would give me a little job to do. He called it a 'task.' I could hardly lift that mallet of his at first, but after a while, I could make buckles and rosettes for harnesses and bridles that could pass his inspection. By the time I was in high school, I was shaping horseshoes out of bars of steel and he was letting me shoe some easy animals. The rough ones he did and made me hold their noses with a twitch. Sometimes, he would even rig up a bunch of ropes and throw the animal down and I would sit on the animal's head. He always told me that if he wanted to take all day, he could have them horses and mules standing still for him, but he couldn't spare the time to baby them.

"You should have seen him handle horses. Him and his friend would drive in a dozen wild horses in late summer: yearlings, year-olds, and older mares. The mares he would first turn loose again. It would take a week, sometimes, for them to run off, because their damn colts were still sucking. When they went dry, they skipped away two or three at a time over those hills."

He waved an arm in the general direction of Rattlesnake Ridge.

"Breaking them was a fall and winter job with the idea that he would sell them as saddle horses and cow ponies in the spring. He would train them in groups all together in the big round corral there." He pointed at a round corral made out of foot-thick logs put together like Lincoln Logs with a snubbing part in the center.

"He had a way with horses that he tried to teach me, but I only learned part. A large part, but a part. In later times, if I had a problem pony I would leave him for a week and that would be the end of it. So anyhow, he would get a halter on them by just following them around talking to them in Indian language. Whispering and blowing his lips. I asked him what he was saying to the horses.

" 'Stand still, you stupid bastard, or I'll kill you.' "

Youngblood and I both chuckled at the joke.

"When he got the halters on, they were special halters with what's called a bosal around their noses, he would tie up one hind foot, with a loop through the bosal and the end of the rope dragging on the ground. These were called sidelines. If the animal stepped on his own rope jumping around, he would throw himself. After a day or two all tied up like that, they would stand still or walk very slowly to water and hay. It usually took two days, sometimes more; next, he would teach them to lead. This he did one or two at a time. He would take a thick cotton rope, tie it in a bowline around their withers so it wouldn't tighten, bring the end of the rope through the loop in the bosal, then fasten it to a truck tire. When the animal backed away, he would think that the tire was chasing him. Those horses kicked and squealed and ran around dragging that tire for half a day before they would learn to move with it. After that, those horses could be led just fine. He would what is called 'sac them out,' wave blankets, handle their feet, trim their hoofs, handle them all over, pull their tails, trim their feet and locks, comb their manes and tails, wash them with a hose and end up putting a saddle on them. They always said he didn't want them to buck even the first time. He would line the head up high so the horse or mule couldn't pull it down. A horse has to have its head down to buck," he added.

I told him that I knew that but he paid no attention to me as he went on.

"He would climb off and on, right, left, over the shoulders and off the rump until the horse got bored with it. Somehow, Dad knew when it was enough. 'How do I know when it is enough?' I asked him. 'You'll know,' he told me, and he was right. Damned guy would hold the horse head talking Indian to it, giving it sugar lumps and blowing his breath into the animal's nostrils until it would stand still. Evidently that's a horse's way of making peace or friends or something. You know, I never saw a single one of those guys really buck. The buckers were the six-year-olds off the reservation. They could buck all right. When I was in high school, we rode them for sport and rodeo competition. I did that a lot, and I was real good at it. Particularly bareback broncos. Want some more good water?"

"Yes I do, thanks."

He disappeared and came back with a glass in each hand.

"Where was I?" he asked when he sat down again.

"You were a boy still in grade school following an Injun around learning."

"Yeah. Oh yeah," he began again. "When I was 10 years old he bought me a single-shot Sears and Roebucks .22 rifle my birthday. We took it out behind the barn and put a lot of bottles on the side of the hill. At first, I couldn't hit a thing. He watched me try for awhile with the barrel waving around because I couldn't hold it still. 'Brady,' he said. 'Let me teach you something. Your eyes are going from the sight to the can and back again. No one can hold a gun steady doing that. Focus on the target alone, and line the sight up in your mind's eye. Practice that.'

"I did and in only a few shots, I could hit my mark every time. The same principle applies with pistols, shotguns, bows and arrows, and slingshots. I never miss," he added with a good-natured snort. "I got so I carried that rifle everywhere I went, I think. There were lots of Blue Grouse around in those days. I got so I could shoot their heads off them clean. We ate a lot of grouse. One day, I was heading out the door with my rifle and ol' Bucky stopped me. 'Let's have beefsteak for dinner,' he said. I got the message.

I shot a lot of cottontails for awhile, before I was nudged back to beef steak." He slapped his knee, enjoying the laugh on himself.

"Well, how about steelhead and salmon and even trout?" I asked. "With the river right here? People come from other states to fish the Gran Rhon. In fact, that's how I ended up here."

"You ended up? Is this your last stop?"

"I don't know."

"Good. A man should never know where he's ended up. Kills imagination."

With his philosophy spoken (which he showed no evidence of living himself), he paused, looking at the trees. Musing. I let him for awhile, but finally I had to ask: "Where was your mother in all this?"

"When she wasn't gone to town or — elsewhere, she sat around drinking beer, smoking cigarettes, reading magazines in her slip and doing nothing. She cooked sometimes, I guess, and kept the place clean. She washed the clothes and painted. She painted the inside and out time and again. At night she let Brady have a poke whenever he wanted to. I could tell he wanted it less and less.

"My ma up and left one day while we — Bucky — that's Emerson — and I — were out shoeing the horses and mules for the rangers. She first took her things and left. She never even left a note. What happened was they let that dude out of jail and he came looking for her and they left. Neither one of us gave a rat's ass, but Bucky got serious. He told me that he would be gone a couple of days. What he did was, he went to a lawyer and got papers drawn up to adopt me. He found out where my ma and the dude were: outside of Asotin. She was served with papers commanding her to appear in court. I had to go, too. We got there an hour early and when she got there with the dude, Bucky ran up and took her aside. He just looked at the dude and I'll tell you, he stayed put where he was. I saw them talking and arguing a little, not very loud really. Then he handed her an envelope. She took it, glanced at me, then went inside with the dude. She signed the adoption papers without even waving at me. I cried and I didn't know why. A guy should have a mother but hell, she was no mother to me except she washed my clothes, made my lunch, put cold rags on my head when I had a fever and sometimes kissed me good-night," he paused, "leaving the scent of her perfume on my nightshirt and a blop of lipstick on my forehead. For a few years, she would send me a birthday card or a Christmas card from California with five dollars in it. Then after a while, that stopped and I never saw her again in my life. Many years later Emerson told me he gave her five thousand dollars he had saved from Indian money over the years. My God, I was sold and bought for five thousand bucks. That's more than anyone could get for me today! He loved his own joke but it made me sad. I never detected a bit of sadness on his part, however.

"You asked me about fishing the Gran Rhon?" he went on. "You know what, it's as good as it ever was right now, despite what the bunny huggers say. At least the Rhon is. I don't know about anywhere else on the Snake. There are big years and not-so-big years. The thing is, people around here go when the fish are in. We don't wait out time beating the water before the run starts or after it is long over. We always had lots of fish, all we could use or give away, but never more. We had it fried, barbecued, Indian smoked, stewed, baked, and boiled. Dad had a way I really liked. He would boil salted water with onion and pickling spices and throw the fish in, then we would eat it cold on pita bread with mayonnaise."

"Sounds good," I said. Then I realized, "You called him 'Dad.' "

"Yeah, I guess I couldn't call him 'Dad' around you until I got to know you."

You don't know me at all, for Christ's sake, I thought without saying anything.

"When the judge handed Emerson the adoption papers, sure was easy then," he said to me. " 'Now you can call Emerson Youngblood your dad, young man. He is one of the finest men I ever knew. See that you deserve it.' Emerson looked up at that judge sitting like a potentate in his black robes and he said, 'He deserves it just because he is he and I love him.' "

The old man kind of choked up on the "I love him" part, but he could hardly get it out when he said it. "I told the judge I loved him, too."

I couldn't stop looking at my shoes.

After a while, he stood up and walked to the porch rail. "When I was 18, I legally changed my name to Youngblood, but from that day in court on, that's what I called myself."

I let him stand there as long as he needed to.

When he came back and sat down again, he looked sort of rested, I would say.

"Ol' Dad and I broke a lot of horses. The ones we thought were useless we just sent into Clarkston to the butcher's. We got fifty cents a pound sometimes. Anyway, because we weeded out the bad ones, we got a name for first-class saddle horses and cow ponies and people came from all over to buy them. We went to a horse auction in Clarkston once and Emerson saw a young Arabian stallion. He had to have it. He paid one thousand dollars for it, a lot of money then, especially for a horse.

" 'What are we going to do with it?' I wanted to know.

" 'We are going to breed those mustang mares with him.'

" 'How?'

" 'Simple. We'll turn him loose with the herd, then shoot all of the males.'

"And that's what we did. You have to understand there were a hell of a lot of wild mustangs then and they were eating good cattle range. The offspring were the finest, prettiest and nastiest critters you ever saw. Damn, they were hard to break.

"Dad had a girlfriend from the reservation named Susan. She had a boy the same age as me. I am not sure who the father was, but it could have been Emerson, that's for sure. When I was twelve, they came to live with us. His name was Russell Faloway. We became the best brothers in the world.

The best friends. And Susan? She smothered me with hugs and wet kisses all the time. The three of them talked Indian all the time at first, but I didn't mind. I picked up a lot of Indian words and meanings, and I taught them proper English when they would listen. Russell had to go to the Indian school in Walla Walla, but he came home every Friday and stayed until Sunday. In high school, he got approved to go to high school where I went in Asotin. Another story," he reflected. "He was smart enough, I think, but I helped him a lot with his schoolwork. He was quite a ways behind at first.

"What I started to say was, we had five of them half mustang half Arabian horses in as three-year-olds to break. Russell, one hell of good hand, especially with a rope, and me had the job. We would go through all the stuff I told you about before but those shit-heads would buck — and I mean *buck* — anyway. So we would tie their heads up high and climb off and on them until they were very quiet before releasing them. It was my turn to climb aboard when Russell decided to play a trick. He made a step loop in the tie down rope that would pull out and release the pony when the pony strained back. Rather than hung tied up tight, the horse had ten feet of slack. I got on, the horse yanked back, the rope came loose and the bronco exploded up in the air, landing on all fours, then, twisting and snorting, reared and sunfished (went belly up). There was one loud craaaack and that horse dropped like he had fallen from an airplane, dead as a stump with a broken neck. I just sat there on top of him. Just a hint of breeze came up whirling a little dust here and there. A little bird chirped somewhere and it sounded rude. Russell looked at me and I looked at him.

" 'Emerson is goin' to be pissed,' he said.

" 'Yeah,' I answered. 'I better go tell him.' It was the first time and only time I was scared to face him. The horse was very pretty, pure black and shiny. It would have drawn $500. Emerson had paddled me once only once when I went swimming in the river where he told me not to go. Sure enough, I got caught in the rapids and had to walk back a quarter of a mile all bruised up from the rocks, cut here and there, and barefoot to boot. He whipped me with the canoe paddle. I screamed like hell, but it didn't hurt a bit and I fooled no one either. So he shook me by the arm. I knew he did it only because I did something so dangerous."

" 'Damn it! You could have been killed!' he yelled. Then kind of quietly, 'What would I do around here without you?'

"Not much of a spanking, but I never did it again. So now I had to go face him. He had told us a hundred times to keep that rope only a foot long until the horse stopped tossing around. Plop, plop, plop went my feet in the dust. I wished I was on the moon or somewhere else. I went to the door and for some damn reason, I knocked rather than going right in. Dad came to the door. I opened it and he stared at me with a wrinkled brow.

" 'What?' he asked.

" 'We killed that black mare,' I blurted out between sobs. That had snuck up on me.

"He looked the longest time. 'Damn, I knew that was a no good son of a bitch,' he exclaimed. 'If you got to kill 'em to break 'em, they ain't no good no-how.' He said a lot of things in Indian that it didn't take no translator to understand.

" 'Come on,' he said pulling on his boots. We went and got the little Ford farm-all tractor. I climbed on the side.

" 'No, you drive,' he said. He opened the gate for me. I ground the gears to kingdom come while he made a big show of plugging his ears and closing his eyes. Off we went with him walking along behind. We took all the gear off the dead pony with our mouths wide open. It was really sad and Russell and I blubbered some.

" 'Quit your damn blubbering and tie that horse on by the neck.' We both ran to it, colliding like bowling pins tumbling over.

" 'For the love of Pete!' said Dad, and he did it himself. He looked back over his shoulder as he drug the hopeless horse away to the ditch way behind the barn.

" 'Quit for the day. Go swimmin' or somethin'.' We gathered up all the gear and did just that. 'We'll get us a couple of bears in a few days,' Emerson Youngblood yelled back at us. We did, too.

"I know that he noticed that the snuffing line was let out ten feet. I think he started to say something about it but changed his mind for some reason known only to him.

"Well, the bears came to the carcass all right, along with the coyotes and buzzards.

"Dad had fixed a car headlight in an apple box along with a car battery. Made a great night light, it did. I have to confess, we skinned a deer once in awhile when we ran out of meat. But, this time, we waited until we heard bears snapping bones. We were hidden in the rocks. Then we jumped up, switched on the light, and Russell and me cut loose with 30-30s. We blew a lot of holes in the ground but we got two nice big bears. The worst part was skinning them and seeing them without their hide. They looked like two naked dead people. That's the only time Indians won't look at them at all.

"Now bear meat is awful, if you ask me. There are big chunks of fat in the meat that are strange, to say the least. We cut them all up into steaks and roasts. Susan cooked some and we gave the rest away to her friends and family. Susan scraped and tanned the two nice hides and we kidded her about being an Indian squaw. They cured hides by urinating on them, rubbing them with the brains and chewing them. I don't know if Susan did all of those things, but she did some of them. She sure had beautiful teeth." Again, he laughed at his own humor more than I did.

"Susan sent the hides off to an old woman on the reservation who turned them into a beautiful pair of chaps for me. Damn near got me killed. If Russell hadn't been there, I would be dead."

"What happened?" I asked.

"Well, we were going for a ride, Russell and me. I put on the chaps and when I went to get on, the cuss, he smelt that bear and went nuts. He reared up and took off, and my foot was caught in the stirrup. I tried to roll and get my foot off but I was drug twenty feet until the horse ran by Russell. He flew out of the saddle and caught a rein with one finger. He held on and stopped the horse or they could have used me for bear bait.

"Dad came running out and kinda chewed me out.

" 'You can't just go at a green broke horse lookin' and smellin' like a damn bear,' he said.

"He took the chaps and laid them across the saddle until the horse stood still. The horses was quivering and sweating and took the hide and left it in the stall with my mount for about a week. Finally the horse didn't pay any more attention to them chaps than he did to a saddle blanket. It took a couple of weeks, though. I made the horse walk around with the chaps across the saddle horn awhile before I got on.

"High school and junior high were together. I had to go into Pomroy to go to school. I was only 13 but I drove in an old World War II Jeep we had. Russell, he went to the Indian school in Walla Walla like I said, but we saw each other almost every weekend.

"There were two brothers in the ninth grade, non-identical twins, I think, who started right out giving me a tough time. They were mean as coyotes. I got pushed and tripped and one day, for no reason, one of them slugged me in the face and gave me a black eye. The teacher, Mr. Klevins, asked me what happened, and I told him I got hit with the tetherball. I was a very tough guy, you understand, but I was awful self-conscious and insecure starting junior high. I knew Klevins didn't believe me but he asked no more. He put ice on it and sat me down for awhile.

"When I got home, Dad took one look at me and said, 'Who hit you?'

"I blubbered a little (I had been holding it back all day), then blurted out the story. He didn't look mad but determined.

"After dinner and chores, he brought out a boxing glove and put it on his hand.

" 'I used to box in amateur matches. I was the champion of the whole Indian tribe. Nez Perce, Yakima, Cayuse, and Palouse. Let me teach you a few things.' I nodded my agreement. 'Let's see you hit the glove as hard as you can.' I swung my arm at it and missed because he pulled it away by a half inch.

" 'See,' he said, 'when you swing like that, it's no good. There is no force behind it my way, but too easy to dodge. Hit straight out like this.' He showed me. 'Shoot your fist out with your shoulder driving it. Like shooting a gun, don't take your eyes off the target. Whatever you do, keep your chin into your chest. Make a fist as tight as you can.' We messed around for an hour or more, me hitting with both hands. I am kind of ambidextrous. Over the next couple of days, he taught me to hit the belly right under the xyphoid. You know, in the solar plexus. I was a natural boxer, but I never liked the sport.

"The next week at school, sure enough, here they came. I carried my lunch in an old wrinkled paper bag that embarrassed me. It seemed like everyone else either had nice new paper bags or lunch boxes with little thermoses in them. Those guys started poking fun at me about my bag and one of them slapped it out of my hands onto the ground.

"Now, old Emerson told me another thing. Hit someone square as you can in the nose. That makes the eyes water like hell and usually the nose bleeds like a hose. Just keep aiming for the nose. My left fist came out like a piston followed by my right before he could react. I spun around and pasted the other guy the same way. There was blood and split flying, I'll tell you. Klevins, the teacher, saw the whole thing and hauled the two jerks with their broken noses off to the office, where a nurse was that day. I picked up my lunch and ate it right there. I learned something big. You know what it was? Revenge can be good for someone. Damn good. Therapeutic despite what the psalm singers say. Revenge isn't all bad.

"The daddy of those two boys was a deputy sheriff and came hauling over to the school with his red light twirling. I wasn't at all frightened or intimidated. I followed him into the office where Klevins was just hanging up the phone.

" 'Who beat my boys up?' he yelled. 'I'm taking them in!'

" 'Well now, Deputy, there was no *them*, it was just him.' He pointed at me standing in the door, a skinny guy about 5'-4" with freckles and spots of blood on my face. The deputy stared at me, disbelieving.

" 'They started it. They were both picking on him and pushing him around. It wasn't the first time, either. I saw the whole thing and I spoke to the superintendent. One more fight out of those boys, and they are expelled. As of now, they are suspended for a week. I suggest you take them to a doctor. Their noses are broken. Oh, and, incidentally, I just spoke to your boss, the sheriff. He agrees with me and he wants to see you.'

"I never had to fight again until college. But that's another story that is neither here nor there.

"I started hanging around with a kid named Charley Artez. His dad was a rodeo star around these parts. That was the days when cowboys did it all. Bulldozing, roping, saddle bronc and bareback bronc riding. Brahma bulls sort of came along later. Tucker Artez was his name. You probably heard of him."

I shook my head no.

"Yep, big Tucker Artez. Biggest star and all around cowboy at the Pendleton Stampede, four years running. Charley and I had that guy as a teacher and a coach. I took to bareback bronc right off. When Russell was home, he went with me and Tucker taught him all he knew about roping, which was plenty. Funny thing, his own kid Charley wasn't very interested at all. He spent his time tinkering with old motorcycles and car engines. At 15, he could fix anything that could be fixed. I remember, he had a collection of three Jeeps that he worked on continuously. Tucker just laughed at him mostly. 'I bet someday they will have a Jeep rodeo,' he said. He was right, too.

"Charley took two of those jeeps apart, then welded them together so they had an engine on both ends. I remember Russell saying it was going to drive him nuts, meaning Charley figuring out he could go two ways at the same time.

"Charley painted that contraption blue with pink polka dots, put whistles, bells, and smoke bombs on it and took it to rodeos as the clown. He was good. He would come driving on in with a clothesline of bloomers on it like he had just been through someone's yard. A bunch of fat ladies in their underwear would chase him and he would get away by going back or forward with his trick car. By the time he was 17 or 18, he had quit school and was going all over the country to fairs and rodeos, making good money.

"I got my first girlfriend toward the end of my third year of high school. Before that, I was just too busy. I lied. I was scared of girls. Anyway, at a barn dance over at the Grange hall, a girl asked me to dance on a ladies' choice thing. Hell, I didn't know how to dance at all, but she was a good teacher. Her name was Geraldine something. She was kind of fat with a round, cute face and tits too big for her size. We danced around a few times, fast and slow, drank too many Cokes, laughed at each other's attempts at joking and held hands a lot. When it was time to go home, I walked her out to her dad's car and while he wasn't looking, she kissed me full on the mouth. Wow! My feet didn't touch the ground all the way home. She went to the same school as me, a year behind me. We hung around some at school but mostly ignored each other until Friday or Saturday night, when I would drive over and pick her up in my Jeep. We usually just drove into town for a hamburger and hung around the hamburger shop with the other kids. On the way home, we started parking, you get the idea, kissing and squirming in the front of an old Jeep. Petting came on pretty quick, as you can guess. I would have her shirt off and her big ones flopping around. Then I started fumbling around under her little skirt. The silky hairs drove me nuts. Her, too. She would hold my arm but not pull it away. It seemed like her eyes were always closed. One time after a full half-hour with my hand under her dress, she suddenly let go of my arm and reached down with both hands and wiggled her panties down. She had had a hold of my dick with her other hand and it was ready to go.

"Try to find a position in a Jeep. It didn't matter because I bounced off her a couple of times and in two seconds covered the silkies with juice. She let out a little screech, pulled her panties up and her dress down and hugged her side of the car. She got real distant. When we got to her house, she just said good-bye and ran in.

"At school, she would hardly look at me. It hurt my feelings, to say nothing of my crippled manly pride. I was pretty glad when she moved away to Lewiston.

"Russell, Charley, and I really loved to fish the Gran Rhon. It is such a beautiful, small river cutting through the hills and paths. The water is almost clear. Just a little blue sometimes. Charley had a big boat he made out of huge truck inner tubes and 4×3/ 4 boards held together by thin ropes through holes in the wood. He was smart. A flat piece of plywood wouldn't give like our deck would. The planks would bend to make up for the pitching of the tubes in rough water. Lots of times, we would leave a truck down at the mouth at the snake river, then drift from the highway down, most of the time dragging an anchor to go slow enough to fish. We caught some beautiful bright silvers and springs, shiny as new bumpers. We also got steelhead that fought like fury. The red stripe showing on their sides could be seen in the sparkling water. The anchor was secured and all was hushed until the fish was brought alongside to get a picture with Charley's Brownie camera. Then we would cut the line right at the hook and let it go. We used hooks that would dissolve in the fish's mouth.

"Canoeing down the river, every now and then we would lose control and go spinning around, whooping and hollering. This happened once and we ended up in a back eddy, bumping on the shore. We sat there laughing at ourselves, eating our lunch and drinking not-too-cold Rainier beers drug along in a sack alongside.

" 'What did I smell?' asked Charley.

" 'Not flowers,' sniffed Russell.

" 'I smell it, too,' I said. 'Let's go see.'

"We tied our vessel up and climbed out on shore.

"It wasn't hard to follow the sweet smell. We went along cautiously through the woods until we could see an open spot up ahead. There were a couple of big vats that the sweet smell was coming from, two large kettles with a propane burner going under them and fluid going through old automobile radiators.

" 'My god, a still!' whispered Charley.

" 'Yeah, sure is,' echoed Russell.

" 'Let's get out of here,' I said. We had heard of people who got shot when they stumbled onto stills unaware. Lightning killed people more ways than one. I saw a guy with a keg and a scruffy beard moving around checking things. We backed up, turned and hightailed it back to our boat and were out of there.

"The county health nurse, whatever she was called, was a friend of Emerson. I heard her talking to him when she stopped to visit at the blacksmith shop.

" 'Something weird going down the river here and in town. People are getting sick as all get-out and it turned out to be lead poisoning,' she said with a *tsk tsk*.

I listened with interest and right away I thought of the moonshine still that we ran into down on the river. The core of an automobile radiator is lead.

Somewhere I had read that moonshiners in the south were killing people with moonshine because of the lead in the automobile radiators they were using as condensor coils. I pictured the still with the tubes running into radiators and out the other side. I really didn't give much of a hoot about someone making whiskey, but this was different. This was after I was out of high school, before I got started in college. Russell and Charley were both gone somewhere so I went down to the sheriff's office by myself.

"I explained to the sheriff what I knew, and he was interested and alarmed. He called the deputy in.

"He said, 'Listen to this.'

"I explained again to the sheriff, and by then, two other deputies.

" 'Where is this still of yours?' demanded Sid. Remember, he was the father of the twins I beat up in junior high. He didn't like me at all.

" 'Listen, Deputy," I replied quickly, staring him in the eye. 'It's not my still.'

" 'Hold on son,' said the sheriff. 'I'll get a map.'

"He looked annoyed, but brought out a map. I studied it carefully.

" 'I can't be sure where it is on the river,' I said. 'We were floating it, fishing.'

"I located a small road on the map that ran off the river road to the river.

" 'It must be on the end of this road,' I pointed out.

" 'That is not much more than a trail. It is all overgrown and there is an iron gate across it. I was just down there. There were signs that the gate had been opened and closed a few times, though.' It was one of the deputies speaking, who acted as a game warden, also.

"The sheriff looked up at me from the map.

" 'Could you find the place from the river in a boat?'

" 'Yes, I think so,' I answered.

" 'Okay, let's set this up tomorrow. Sid, you take — wh-what's your name?'

"Brady Youngblood."

" 'Take Mr. Youngblood down the river in the boat and we will come in from the road.' he looked to his other deputy. Sid did not look pleased. 'Sid, I know you can manage the float boat, so you do it.'

"Sid shut up. Arrangements were made. I was to meet Sid at the launching ramp at 6 a.m. It would take 45 minutes, I figured, to reach there, so the other guys would go in from the road about the same time.

"When I got to the ramp in the morning, the boat was in the water and Deputy Sid was waiting impatiently. I said hello. He didn't answer. Asshole. We made it down the river to where us guys had come in with the fish in about half an hour. We tied the boat up and made it through the woods to where the clearing was. Sid was smiling when he saw the still working away. There was a big guy there poking around with a big paddle in the vats. He stopped suddenly, looked up in the direction of the road in. He had heard something, it was obvious. He dropped the paddle and ran over to a tire where a single-shot shotgun was leaning. He took a few steps up toward the road.

Sid stepped out in the open with me right behind him.

" 'Halt and stay put. You are under arrest. Put down the gun,' Sid was screaming, but hadn't even drawn his pistol. The man turned, pointed his gun and shot. Sid let out a half scream and slumped forward. I was right behind him. I was aware that a shot had torn through the side of my coat and it was stinging. The moon shiner was frantically opening his shotgun to push in another shell. His hands were shaking and he was having trouble. Sid was bent over double on his face. Without thinking, I pulled his pistol from his holster, a big revolver, and pulled the hammer back. Neither of us said anything. The man had been able to reload. He was smirking as he started to bring the shotgun up. I shot him right in the chest, breaking the shotgun up as the bullet entered his chest. He stared in disbelief then fell over backward. Another guy with a big bushy beard came running up from inside a tent. Obviously he had heard the shots. He had a 30-30 Carbine in his hands and was looking around wide-eyed. When he saw me with the pistol and his partner laying face up, he dropped his rifle and put his hands up.

" 'Don't shoot, don't shoot,' he pleaded.

"Hell, I was shaking so bad I couldn't have hit the broadside of a barn. The sheriff and his other deputy came running down the road. The sheriff came running up to Sid while his deputy handcuffed the bushy-faced moonshiner.

"Sid was rolled up on his side, moaning. The sheriff and I got him on his back. Four holes were shot though his shirt above his belt to his chest.

" 'Damn. 2-0 buckshot. You hurt, son?'

"I started to say, 'I ain't your son, but thought better of it and pulled up my own coat and shirt. A bleeding crease was in my sides. I held a bandanna on it.

" 'Didn't go in,' I said.

" 'What the hell happened?'

"I told him. He looked annoyed.

" 'You shot him?' he pointed to the dead man.

" 'Yes, he was about to shoot me,' I said defensively. He didn't say anything to me.

" 'Damn it, Karl, get the car in here now. Let's get Sid to the hospital.'

" 'What do I do with *him?*' the deputy asked.

" 'Fuck him,' the sheriff said as he ran over and handcuffed bush-face to a tree.

" 'Get moving.'

"That's about the end of the moonshine story," the old man said. "Look at this scar." He pulled up his shirt. "It was a goodly scar, all right. After a lot of pictures were taken, that still was dismantled to pieces and the lead poisoning stopped." He looked like he was enjoying a private joke. "Deputy Sid has been nice to me ever since."

"Well," I said. "I had better get out of your hair. I just wanted to meet you and talk to you." I started to get up.

"You're not in my hair. Stay and have supper."

"What are we having?" I asked.

"Blue grouse and fried potatoes. Tomatoes and cucumbers from the garden."

"Talked me into it," I said.

We talked some more — a lot more — as I helped him light a fire in the wood stove and fix supper.

"I don't drink," he said out of the blue.

"Neither do I," I lied.

He had some ice tea made in the sun, filled with lemon. It was good stuff.

"See that ridge there?" he asked, waving his arm behind him.

"Yes."

"It is called Rattle Snake Ridge."

"It is."

"Yep, it is for good reason."

I could tell another story was coming.

"When I was 16, I think, I was up there cutting wood for the cook stove. I stepped over a log and — wham — I get hit in the leg. At first it was like getting hit with a stick and then it started to tingle and burn. Then, it started to hurt like the fires of hell. I let out a girlish scream and Dad came running over. He knew right away what happened. He laid me down on a soft grassy spot and told me not to move a muscle.

"He took off my belt and twisted up a tourniquet just at my knee. I hurt so bad I couldn't even scream. You know, it's not the poison that kills you from a snake bite, at least not a rattler, it's the shock from the pain. Emerson ran over to his truck and brought back his pistol. I thought he was going to kill the snake. He ripped open my pant leg with his knife then cut a piece out of my leg where the bite marks were. You know, from the side." He pulled his pant leg up and showed me a big dent with a shiny scar over it.

"Blew the poison away. Dad sucked that wound fifty times and spit blood all over the place while I laid there covered with sweat and shivering. All kinds of lights and shooting stars went off in my head and it was hard to breathe even though I was panting.

" 'Am I going to die?'

" 'Someday, but not today,' quipped old Emerson.

"He released the tourniquet from time to time and that first made the pain worse. He made me lay there for a long time without moving around. Theory is, that keeps the poison from being pumped around. Panic kills a lot of snake-bitten people. If a person has sores in his mouth, the venom can get into the system of someone sucking at the bite and kill them dead. Emerson knew that, too, so he rinsed his mouth out after each suck and more. You know about rattlesnake venom?" he asked. Without waiting for an answer, he continued on.

"It is a very stable chemical. You can boil it or freeze it and it stays the same. People have got flat tires from snakes. You are supposed to cut the head off and bury it when you kill a rattler. I saw a guy stick a piece of wood in just a head once and that mouth chomped it right down by itself. I saw it."

I had no reason to doubt him.

"Birds get at the head and it kills them. That's another reason to bury it. One time Russell had a brand spankin' new $65 pair of boots. A snake hit it above the ankle without getting Russell. He said he could feel the boot getting all hot inside. Emerson took the boot off and threw it in the campfire. I thought Russell was going to bawl. Sooner or later, that poison would get Russell. Never goes away. Never. Anti-venom used to be made from horse serum. Now it's cows. Serum sickness killed more people than the snakebites. I used it a lot on dogs. They never got serum sickness. Funny thing, pigs eat rattlesnakes. I don't know how they get away with it. If they get hit in the fat, I guess. The poison is absorbed so slow it doesn't get them."

He was really enjoying the talk and I was enjoying listening.

"Stay away from Rattlesnake Ridge."

"I will."

"Part of it is on your property."

"I will donate that part to the Catholic missions."

After dinner, the old guy and I sat on the porch again. He lit up a homemade corncob pipe.

"You are a veterinarian?"

"Yep, sure am. I work about half day twice a week for some of my old friends. What do you do?"

"I'm an actor and writer," I replied.

He didn't bat an eye. This conversation was about him.

"Did you ever see a doctor or go to the hospital with your bite?" I asked.

"Nope. Never did. My leg swelled all up but went down and I was good as new in awhile."

"How did you get to vet school?" I asked.

"Emerson asked me what I wanted to do after high school. I said I wanted to be a veterinarian.

" 'So why don't you, then?' he said to me.

" 'It costs a lot of money.'

" 'I have money for you,' he told me. 'Indian money. I saved it all.'

"I was 18 and had made my own money for awhile.

" 'That's your money,' I said.

" 'Nope,' said Emerson. 'I saved it for you.'

" 'What will you do to retire?'

" 'Hell, I'll never retire. If you want, I'll just go back to the reservation.' He thought that was real funny, but I also knew he was serious. I did all right in college. I got along fine. Emerson paid for tuition and books, and I got a job in the commissary for room and board. Besides, some rich old cowboy came up with a rodeo scholarship. First of its kind, I think. Since I was the best bronc rider around, I got it. Not much, as I recall, but I always had a car and spending money. Russell had a full ride to school as an Indian. There are so many plans available to them — Indians, I mean — that just go begging. Lots of reasons why, none of them reasons any damn good. Russell went to Oregon and studied farming agriculture. He won enough money roping in rodeos for his spending money."

"How about your other friend, Charley?" I asked, because I really wanted to know.

The question seemed to make him a little uncomfortable and didn't bring an immediate answer.

"Charley was one hell of a guy. I told you, how he was a rodeo clown, but he was a guitar playing, banjo playing, yodeling, singing entertainer as well. From the get go. He was good, you probably heard of him if you know anything about western music. Called himself Charley Pine."

I told the old guy that I didn't really like western music.

"Why?"

"It's all filled with cliches and lamenting about shit. Beer, divorce, jobs and old dog Skip."

"It used to be that way. Now it's screaming and yelling I can't stand either. After a pause, he said, "You left out cheating and pick-up trucks."

This time I didn't acknowledge him.

"So Charley had a band. He called it a group. Charley Pine and the Ridge Runners. They were successful all over Washington, Oregon, Idaho and into Montana and Wyoming. He wanted to go to Nashville in the worst way and, kind of thanks to me, he did."

"Thanks to you?"

"After the first year of college, I met a girl from Moses Lake named Linda Lou. I met her at a rodeo party. You know we had great big boot-stampin' beer parties after the rodeo. They were really something. I looked forward to them a lot more than competing." He enjoyed his comment.

"Well, Linda Lou was sitting up front by herself so I just went and sat down by her."

" 'Can I buy you a beer?'

" 'No, I don't drink.'

" 'A Coke. You drink Coke?'

" 'Yes, that would be all right.'

"Well, she wasn't a Mormon. They didn't drink Coke in those days, only after they bought stock in it. It didn't matter anyhow, because I couldn't get a waitress over with that crowd and didn't want to leave her long enough to go to the bar. She told me she was a student at Whitman in Walla Walla. She was studying music and she really wanted to be a singer. I asked her, 'How would you like to sing with this band? Here? Now?' She just looked at me with big blue eyes and her dimples increased. I think I fell in love with her right then. I know I did. She just said, 'yeah' like it was, of course, impossible. It was Charley's band. So I took her by the hand and led her onstage off to one side and waved Charley over when he was done with his piece.

" 'Charley, this is Linda Lou. She wants to sing with you.'

"Charley just looked at her very kindly.

" 'You sing?' he asked.

" 'Yes.'

" 'You any good?'

" 'I sure am.'

" 'Okay, Linda Lou, what do you know cold?'

" 'What about *I am Lost in Love with You*?'

"She was good. She sang four songs. Sometimes they sang together, Charley and Linda. They pleased and surprised everyone with *He Taught Me How to Yodel*. They sang it together like they had rehearsed a hundred times. I was absolutely thrilled.

"That summer, Linda and I spent all our free time together. She worked in a bank in Asotin and sang all over with the band on the weekends. I went to as many as I possibly could. Shows, I mean. When we were out of town, we stayed together. She was so affectionate. Not the right word — she made love to me like she was singing her favorite song. We told each other we loved one another, and I really meant it. She did, too. At first. gradually, I saw cobwebs growing. 'Let me sleep, I'm tired.' 'I have cramps.' 'Don't you think of anything else?' I got kind of desperate. I just ached for her.

" 'Let's get married.'

" 'Are you kidding?'

" 'No. I mean soon.

" 'I don't want to get married. I want to go to Nashville with my own songs.'

" 'I'll go with you.'

" 'No.'

" 'Just no?'

" 'I don't want to marry you.' she said.

"That was plain, but it was hard for me to see, let alone accept. I actually had physical pain in my chest."

I understood; I had had that pain also.

"The band, or the group — they called themselves Lindy Lou and Charley's Ridge Runners —
got a big gig at the Puyallup Fair in Seattle. They did
great. I saw them when the came in on the train at
Clarkston. Linda Lou was holding Charley's hand
and every now and then they kissed each other. I just
felt numb. Desperate and numb. Charley saw me
and ran over to me, leaving the girl fussing self con-
sciously with her purse.

" 'Hey, Youngblood. What are you doing here?'

" 'I came to give you guys a ride,' I mumbled.

" 'That's good of you, but I have my own car.'

"It was obvious then that Linda was with him.

" 'Hey, Youngblood, we got a chance at Nashville. Can you believe it? Linda's songs.'

"Linda looked away from me as Charley ran
over and took her hand.

" 'Congratulations,' I said, and turned and left,
and left part of my heart there and didn't look back."

He sat still gazing 'half way.' I squirmed around
embarrassed and afraid the man would get more
emotional than he was. He didn't, and I was glad. He
put out his pipe and continued on.

"I went back to college at the end of the summer
and I did well. When I came home for Christmas,
there was a 13-year-old Indian girl living with us.
Her name was Daisy. She was a Nez Perce from
across the river and her mother was Suzy's sister's
kid. Suzy's sister was all messed up with alcohol and
pot. She just disappeared one night. No one ever saw

her again. So, we had her. Emerson had a daughter and I had a little sister sort, anyway. She was a cute little shit with kind of a round face, big black eyes, full pouty lips, shiny black hair, and a single dimple. She seemed to giggle all the time and I think it was mostly because she was so glad go be with us. Her drunken mother had made her life pure hell. That kid followed me around everywhere. She would look so sad anytime I went anywhere that I started to take her with me. I mean everywhere. Fishing, to town, to the store, to visit and even to go hunting. I gave her my old .22. She got to be a good shot. She loved to go with me to rodeo practice. I went three times a week at least. A guy gave me a little black wild mustang, and Daisy and I trained it together. She got bucked off a bunch of times, but always got back on. She got that pony tamed down into a fine riding horse. (Emerson helped out a lot.) She rode bareback, ' 'cause I am an Indian.' She rode that critter at least once a day and sometimes more. I remember Suzy telling her to stop riding bareback with a dress on because she was wearing out her underpants. She started developing little breast blossoms pretty soon. I think she was a little behind because of poor nutrition until she came to live with us. Anyhow, she got self-conscious and starting acting round shouldered. I thought it was funny at first, but gradually I saw how sensitive she was. So one day I just up and told her, 'Daisy, you know what? You got the cutest little boobies in the world.' She didn't know whether to laugh or hit me. She smiled all over her face and hit me anyway. That ended the whole problem right there.

"When I went back to college at Washington State, after Christmas semester break and spring break, Daisy was getting to be a little lady in a lot of ways. Not just physical ones, though that was obvious, but more subtle ways, too. Like, she flirted with me in a way that was awkward at first but became less so. She seemed 15 going on 20 sometimes, then just a silly little girl at others. One day she said to me, 'I am going to marry you.' I blushed like hell and I can't say I wasn't damn flattered, or something. Not so comfortable.

"Let me shorten things up a little," the old man said with a sigh.

Why start now? I thought without saying anything.

"It went like this. I got through vet school in two years. Takes four now. I rode in lots of rodeos, amateur ones, to keep amateur standing. I rode in college rodeos all over the west, sometimes to Oklahoma and Texas. I was good and I knew it. I was on my way to being the college bareback bronc champion. It was a big aim of mine.

"I still came home all I could because I liked seeing Dad, Susan, and Daisy. They always seemed so glad to see me and the love they gave me was very easy to give back. All three came to the rodeos I was in that they could get to."

He paused for a long time now and twisted in his seat. Something uncomfortable coming up, I thought. I was right.

"Daisy started running around with a bunch of kids from her high school that, we'll say, I didn't approve of. They were probably no worse than I was. I don't know. She started having less time for us — Emerson, Susan, and me — and she was barely around. She told Emerson that she didn't want to be adopted. It hurt his old red feelings pretty bad but I guessed it was because she didn't want to be my sister. I didn't want her to either. I never would have told her so. But I didn't want her to be my sister either. When she graduated from high school, she was gone. She headed for California to go to university in San Francisco. She had an Indian scholarship and got spending money from her aunt and uncle and the part-time job she had at a bank.

"Emerson, Susan, and I missed her a lot. She wrote and called less and less, which is the way it is supposed to be, I guess, and Susan just continued to write her every week the way it is supposed to be, I think. She called maybe once a month and always left a number we could never reach her at. She was always kind of excited because she had a part in a play or a musical or was doing a commercial on television. That didn't surprise me a bit. She always was an actress.

"I had one more year to go in vet school when the college rodeo championships came to Lewiston, Idaho. I was ready; pumped up, excited and ready. Like I said, I was good and I knew it. I had a girlfriend then named Sandy, who was the rodeo queen. We were close, I guess you would call it, but a long way from being in love. She had been out and met Emerson and Susan. She liked them (who didn't?) and they really liked her. She would kick her boots off ask for a sandwich if she was hungry and make herself at home. They liked that.

"The day came for the big ride. I called home that morning and Susan answered."

" 'Are you coming to the rodeo?'

" 'I don't think so. Emerson isn't feeling well. He has a bad cough and his chest hurts.'

" 'Does he have a fever?'

" 'I think so. He feels hot, but the thermometer we had broke.'

" 'You should get another one,' I said sharply. I was concerned. Emerson didn't get sick.

" 'He is sleeping now. He was up most of the night coughing. I don't want to wake him up. Why don't you call after the rodeo? Emerson's friend Dr. Moffet is coming by this afternoon.'

" 'He is a horse doctor!'

" 'He treats lots of people, too. He has delivered a lot of the babies around here.' She seemed defensive, so I let it go. 'I think he will fill him with a lot of penicillin,' she added.

" 'I guess that is all right. Penicillin is penicillin. Horse, dog, or man.' I hung up a little worried.

"My ride came up late in the go around. I drew a big roan with one blue eye and one brown eye. He had a Roman nose, pig ears, and a constant sneer on his lips. He had the big quarters that I liked to see, but kind of high withers, which I didn't like to see. He was kicking hell out of the chute to begin with. It took three guys to get my bucking rig around him. Sandy gave me a worried kiss before I lowered myself aboard. They tightened the bouncing strap around his haunches. He went crazy. I nodded. The gate flew open and out we went. That nag flew out. Lit on all fours, reared, bucked, twisted, snorted, climbed the air, sun fished, and hunkered. I held on with all my strength, pulling my ass down and leaning back as far as I could. I spurred his heck without stopping. The horn sounded. Eight seconds. I had ridden him out and I knew it was one hell of a ride. A championship ride. The pick-up man rode up and unsnapped the bucking strap. It didn't seem to make a hell of a lot of difference. Then, really without thinking, I waved the pick-up man away and jumped off Indian style. No pick-up man! I lit on my feet, then went ass over teakettle in the dirt. Somehow my damn hat had stayed on so I took it off and waved to the crowd. People came from all over the place, slapping me on the back and calling me champ. I like to have broken my face smiling. I felt like a million bucks and I don't mean all wrinkled and green. That evening, they presented me with what I wanted more than anything at the time, a big, bold, silver belt buckle with gold inlay that said *Champion*. Gosh, I was proud.

"Before we went to the rodeo dance that evening, I called home and got Emerson on the phone. I asked him how he was feeling and he said much better, except for the penicillin shot in the ass. He said that hurt more than his chest.

" 'Hey, Dad, should I come out? I have to show you something.'

" 'I know, a belt buckle with *Champion* written on it.'

" 'How did you know?'

" 'Why, my God, I was on the phone with Sandy while you were jumping off. Indian style.'

" 'Yeah, Dad; Indian style.'

"There was silence on both ends.

" 'I am proud of you, Son.'

"It was the first time he ever called me 'Son.'

"I choked a little but croaked out, 'I am proud that you are my dad. I love you, you know.'

" 'Yeah, I know, and I love you, too.'

" 'I was afraid I would have to come out there with a shovel,' I said as lightly as I could.

" 'Naw, I'm better. You just go to the dance with Sandy and have yourself a good time.'

" 'I will come out in the morning first thing. Tell Susan hello. See you in the morning.'

"What a party, what a dance. What fun. What beer. How many compliments. How many slaps on the back. How many people calling me champ. How many kisses from pretty girls I didn't even know.

"Sandy and I had a good time. She wanted to stay with me, so I let her." He laughed a good laugh. "Let her, hell. I begged her."

With that, he got serious. "I went out to the place, it was already 10 a.m. and my head still hurt. I had my buckle in my hand as I went through the door.

"Susan was sitting in the corner rocking back and forth with a shawl over her head, making a quiet high pitched whimpering sound.

"I knew. God, I knew, and my heart broke into a million pieces."

The old man wiped his eyes and I wiped mine. I couldn't look up and neither could he. Presently, he was able to speak again.

"There were a lot of people I never knew at the funeral. Lot of Indians, but a lot of other people, too. Everyone that he knew. I buried him with the big silver belt buckle with golden inlay that said *Champion* around his waist. I never rode in another rodeo."

Book II

The Short End

"I graduated from vet school, passed my license and set up town there where you see the office. Mostly, at first, I went around a lot doing large animal stuff. At first, I even had to show a few horses to make a buck.

"Susan went back to live on the reservation. She lived until she was 86. She told me she still loved Emerson when she died."

"What happened to Daisy?"

"I'm getting to that," he said sharply.

"Sandy married a lawyer from Lewiston who became a judge. She was happy and I was happy for her. I could have —"

He didn't finish.

"Charley and Linda Lou did real well," he went on. "They made records I hear on the radio today. The folk music boom really came at a good time for them. They came back to Clarkston one time. My god, 50 years ago. We were all about 45, I guess. Somewhere around there."

I tried to do the arithmetic in my head, but it wasn't any good.

"Well, Charley looked fine. His wrinkles looked distinguished and he still had a full head of wavy hair that was in the pretty stage of changing colors. He had a little potbelly, not much, a little extra chin, not much, and looked like he spent time in the sun.

"Linda Lou looked like she had smoked too many cigarettes. She had wrinkles around her mouth and her eyes that she looked like she had borrowed from a walnut. She was up 50 pounds, 20 of which were in her tits, and the rest in her ass. I'm not being nice, am I? I probably didn't look too good myself. But, nevertheless. Funny how things work out."

Sure is, I thought.

"What about Daisy?" I asked.

"I'm getting there. Russell got a degree in agriculture and went to work for the Nez Perce tribe down in the valley where they got some of their land back. We stayed good friends over the years. He died at 87. I miss him still. There is a park down on The Dalles with his name on it. He was one damn good Indian." He paused. "You want to know about Daisy, don't you?"

"I sure do," I answered.

The old man sat back in his chair and ran his hand through his ample white hair. He had a little habit of doing that.

"I was in practice here about three years. More I think," he started. "Most of my work was driving to farms and ranches to take care of sick cows. I castrated a million of them, I think. Horses, too. I never liked castrating horses. Anyhow, I came home one night and a brand-new white Volkswagen beetle was parked right at my front door. In those days, I never bothered to lock the door. Anyone could kick it in anyway. She was inside waiting for me. She had made coffee and there were a lot of groceries on my kitchen table. She was in her old bedroom. I just knew who it was.

" 'Daisy?' I called out quietly.

"She came out and without a word, she put her coffee down and came over to me in the damnedest hug I ever had. She was crying softly to herself. I realized I had never seen her cry before. We just held each other a little while there. Between us, a feeling inside us passed to each other. Feelings of life lived, pain, regret, sadness, disappointment, some loneliness. Intense feelings tempered by accomplishment, but very little... free floating... uh — unencumbered happiness. You know what I mean?"

"Yes, sir. I certainly do."

" 'Brady? Do you ever think about me?' she asked.

" 'Yes, Daisy, I do. Every day, I think.'

" 'What do you think?'

" 'I think — I thought you that you were someone else. Lost to me. A page turned in a book. Not just someone lost, but something lost. Like being young.'

" 'Did you care?'

" 'It broke my heart, but a lot of things have and I was waiting for it to heal.'

" 'Did it heal, Brady?'

" 'No.'

"We separated then, and she went into the kitchen calling after her, 'Come. I brought steaks. I want to fix you your supper.'

"I was kind of amused because she called it supper rather than dinner. Down home. That simple thing brought out a warm feeling of affection that had been gone a long time. I helped her peel and fry potatoes while she made coleslaw. She remembered it had always been my favorite salad. I lit up the charcoal barbecue on the porch; as usual, I used enough starting fluid to burn the house down. She laughed when the fire flamed up and I fell off the porch getting away. It was good to hear her laugh, but I wondered what I looked like with my eyelashes singed off.

"After we ate our supper, we sat out on the porch in the gathering dusk. The sunset was bright red and orange. The birds had not stopped their bedtime serenade yet. It was time to ask. It was time to talk. Daisy looked older, of course. There were fine lines at the corners of her eyes, but few other wrinkles. The skin of her neck and face were darker but smooth and tight. Her breasts were firm and pointed. Perfect breasts. Man-made. I remembered her little flowers. I almost said something, but thought better of it, and shut up. Her backside had more substance, but because her waist was slim, she looked awfully good.

" 'You know where I have been, Daisy. Where have you been?'

" 'You never got married, Youngblood?'

" 'No.'

" 'Have you had lots of lady friends?'

" 'Yes, lots.'

" 'Why didn't you get married?'

" 'I never found anyone who would have me, I guess. Anyone that I wanted anyway. Have you been married?'

" 'No, not really.' Sounded like a lie.

" 'Why?'

" 'I never found anyone that would have, who would have me.' That sounded like another half-truth but I thought it best not to pursue it.

" 'You did good, acting,' I said. 'I saw you on television a couple of times. You were in a commercial for ponybras.'

" 'Pantyhose.'

" 'Panty something.'

" 'I have done a lot of theater down in California. I like live theater best. I never got to do any real movies, anyway.'

" 'Real movies? Like porno?'

" 'No! Like *Lassie, Come Home.*'

" 'Oh.'

" 'Anyway, I quit.'

" 'You quit?'

" 'I just quit.'

" 'Why?'

" 'It was a fast life. Pot, booze, rock and roll.'

"She left out the sex and we both knew it.

" 'I'm glad you are here.' I started to ask her why, but she interrupted me.

" 'I'm just getting over an operation,' she said. I waited.

" 'They took everything out. My uterus and ovaries. I had a pelvic abscess. My boyfriend, the one I was living with, brought it home to me.'

"She hadn't mentioned she had a live-in. Strangely, I was slightly disappointed in her. None of my business, though, I thought.

" 'Now I take hormones and I feel normal. Normal as I can without —' she let it slide.

" 'So you left?'

" 'Yes, so I left.'

" 'Are you really all right, Daisy?'

" 'No!' She started crying again. I gathered her on my lap and her tears ran down my neck. I kissed her on the top of her head and stroked her beautiful shiny black hair. I kissed her forehead and her cheeks. I stopped short of her quivering lips. But I wanted to kiss them as well.

" 'Daisy, stay here. As long as you want.' She did, too, about 26 years.

"I guess I knew it. I guess I knew I loved her since the day when she was a little girl. When she said she was going to marry me and she wouldn't let Emerson adopt her because she would be my sister. We got married in about a month, as I recall. Russell came up from Oregon with Susan, and you know who else? Charley came. Charley came without Linda Lou. I never asked why she didn't come, but I think I knew.

"That's about it. We adopted a boy and a girl. All grown and gone now. Emerson is an English professor at the University of Washington. Daisy, my daughter, hates her name but that's what it is. She teaches kindergarten in Olympia. They are both happily married. I think, anyway. I got six grand children that come over to drive me nuts in the summer."

"Do you hear from your children?"

"Hell, yes. They drive me nuts, too! Why do you think people talk to older folks like they are kids?"

"I don't know, but you are right."

"God, they both check up on me twice a week. I would hate to have their phone bill."

I knew better. He was proud and he wouldn't mind having the phone bills at all.

"Daisy?"

"She slipped over in her sleep in a nursing home after she broke her hip. She was 85."

"How long ago, Youngblood?"

"A hundred years," was his answer.

Dark now. He just asked me my name and what I did, so I never told him anything other than that I was a writer. It was his story, not mine.

"Tell you what, Brady Youngblood. This one acre here, the house and barn and all, I am deeding it back to you to live on as long as you want."

"You mean until I die."

"Yes, I guess I do mean that."

"It will be another twenty years, you know."

"I know that, but what the hell."

"Yeah. What the hell. I accept," he said.

Treasure of the Indios

Chapter 1

Michael wasn't surprised by the events, but the timing. Four o'clock in the morning, Patricia came home with her clothes and hair all rumpled up and her lipstick kissed off. She came directly into the bedroom where he lay awake, switched on the room's indirect lighting system, inadvertently turning on the CD sound system as well. She fumbled around, attempting to push the buttons that turned the sound off, gave up and headed to the bathroom with a rush. Michael sat up in bed, lit a cigarette and waited for her. When she came out, she spoke not a word, went into her side of the walk-in closet and lugged out a suitcase.

Michael looked up at her without surprise.

"Are you going somewhere?" he asked flatly.

"That's a stupid question. Why else would I be packing?" she replied in a matter-of-fact fashion.

"Where are you going?"

"None of your business. I'm leaving."

"Oh, I see. Are you mad at something?"

She stopped and stared at him.

"Don't you get it? I'm leaving here and you. I want out. I want a divorce," she blurted.

"Patricia, mellow out. You're drunk."

"I am not drunk."

"Well isn't this a hell of a time to just up and leave. Has something happened?" He left it hanging.

"Yes, something has happened. I realize I don't love you now and I probably never did." She continued packing.

"This you tell me after twelve years together? At four in the morning?"

She stopped short and glared at him. "We should never have gotten married in the first place. We couldn't even get along while we were living together. It's my fault, too," she said a little more kindly. "I don't know why we thought things would change by making it legal."

Michael looked down to put on his slippers. "I think I know who your lover is. You think Bob is going to be your soul mate? He has been married twice before, you know. He has teenage kids, for Christ's sake."

"That's more than we have."

"Who the hell's fault is that?" She didn't answer.

"Do you have a lawyer? I am afraid that's another dumb question. Knowing you, I'll bet you do."

"No, I don't, damn it," she paused. "I have an appointment to talk to Harold on Friday."

"Harold, my golfing buddy? I'll be damned."

"His wife is my best friend."

"So what," he exclaimed. She continued to pack putting her toilet articles in a carry-on overnight bag.

"Why do you have to wait until Friday? That's a week away."

"He is in trial. In Tacoma," she added.

Michael then got off the bed and began to pace around the room, rubbing at his face with his hands.

"God," he said. "I didn't want this."

"You think I did? I have given you twelve of the best years of my life."

"For the love of heaven. That sounds like a cliché from a soap opera 'The Best Years of My Life!' Shit, oh dear. Where was I in all that? How about my life?"

"You were in the school while I marched my ass off. Then — then," she paused, "all you did was work. You left me then. Alone all the time looking for something to do with myself." She looked like she might cry, but she didn't. She looked tough as whang leather instead.

"No wonder," she said quietly to herself.

No wonder she found someone else, he thought. *That's what she meant to say*. He let it go without acknowledgment.

"You're making a mistake, Pat. Bob is a woman-izing asshole."

She responded by closing her bags in a huff.

"He is about as sincere as a fucking… I don't know what."

Pat put on her coat rapidly.

"Do you need help out with your bags?" Michael asked, not unkindly.

"I'll manage myself," she said with disdain. She grabbed the bags and walked out of the room without a backward glance, slamming the door behind her with her foot. The front door she left open. He watched her load the bags into the trunk of her Mercedes and pull away with a squeal of rubber.

Michael stood there awhile and bawled a little. Then anger moved in where such disappointment had been before.

Chapter 2

Saturday and Sunday went by at a snail's pace. He tried to drink, but made him feel worse in every way.

Monday, he began to work out his own plans.

He went to the bank where his credit card was and wrote a check for the maximum cash advance he could get: twelve thousand dollars. *That's ironic*, he thought. He was surprised he didn't need his wife's signature, because she also was on the account. He bought a safe deposit box at another bank and put the money in there, all except $1,000, which he kept in his pocket.

Michael's assets were held by his professional service corporation. All of them. his house, his office, his accounts receivable, his automobile, his insurance. Being a professional service corporation, his was the only signature required, and, as a matter of fact, the only one that could be used.

It took only two days to complete his transactions.

The two cars were mortgaged to the max. His house was mortgaged to the max. His professional business line of credit was maxed. His insurance was borrowed back to its base value. All of his stocks were sold off and he borrowed the maximum value on his pension plan that was legal. He sold his golf cart. He pawned his wife's jewelry she was dumb enough to leave behind. He sold all his furniture to a hustler and had it cleared out in a day. He then sold his riding lawn mower. Nothing much was left at home. A bed, a chaise lounge from the yard, a television set, a refrigerator, and a washer and dryer were about all that was left. His prized collection of tools he put into storage. He changed the locks on the doors and garage and when he got all his monthly bills together — telephone, utilities, gas and electric — he put them through his shredder and then threw the shredder in the garbage.

He had told his office staff to cancel all surgeries and office visits and look for other jobs. They were shocked, but they did as they were told. He paid them each a month in advance and told them to do something with the records. Some storage company that would give them out when asked, for a price that would handle expenses and make them a nice profit for copying as well

All of the money put together was put in an off-shore numbered account in the Cayman Islands. It held over 3 million dollars, plus the twelve thousand he kept in cash in the lock box.

Friday, Michael bought a one-way ticket to McAllen, Texas, and left with four large suitcases (brand new) filled with his clothes. That, incidentally, was the last of his available credits on his MasterCard.

He was pensive and quiet on the plane trip to Texas. The bloody Mary tasted good and felt good, so he had two.

Am I vindictive, he wondered to himself. "Hell, yes," he replied under his breath. On he thought. *If*

only she had come to me and told me she was as unhappy as all that. He knew something was wrong, of course, but like in the past, he had simply waited until she came to him in a bucket of blues. He would understand. They would make love then go two weeks to Hawaii or Mexico or the Bahamas, where shortly things would be all right again. For awhile. Not to be that way this time. For three months he had heard her whispering on the phone. She began coming home late at night after "meeting with the girls." She bought new clothes, purses and shoes (which Michael carried gleefully to good will after she left).

Caller ID revealed who the calls were to. Michael never did like or respect good old accountant-boy Bob. Now he despised him. What a waste of time despising him, he knew. It was both their fault. Fault? What a meaningless, hollow concept. People do what they have to do. Sometimes they just go along with things, never considering the consequences. They look for something else. They just look for something else, period, and literally just aren't themselves at all. Reason and judgment go with such discontent. Then the conscience goes right behind, ushered in by recklessness. Someday people must stop, weigh things, judge themselves and often carry on looking for forgiveness. Understanding? Not appropriate at all. Forgiveness is the word.

What is the greatest attribute of a person? Michael mulled over in his mind. Someday I'll know the answer to that. Self-sacrifice causes self-pity. Generosity seeks a reward. Honesty can be cruel, while deceit can be sparing. Religiosity is for people weakened by their need for control of the universe and other people in senseless repetitiousness and self-serving ritual.

You know, Michael thought to himself, *under it all I am optimistic that people are generally good and the world is filled with wonder for us all. There is a tomorrow. Next week I will be 45, that's young. I am healthy, adventurous (although adventurousness has been on a back burner for awhile).* He smiled as he patted himself on the back mentally. He came from a poor and horribly dysfunctional family and made 3 million dollars, became an M.D., a surgeon and a fellow in the American College of Surgeons. *I have a lot of successes. Too bad the major failure had been as a husband. Stop! Don't blame yourself! You did the best you could. You did what you had to do. My God, maybe Patricia did the best she could. Maybe she did what she had to do under the circumstances.* He knew in his heart he loved her and wished very hard that things were different.

But Bob? He hated that nobody prick whom he had heard so many times bragging about his conquests. Let him stick his dick in a pencil sharpener, the bean counting fart. After this, his second divorce, he couldn't have much money left. Alimony, child support, mortgages and living expenses. Well, he would have himself a great surprise because old Michael Hart wasn't going to support the lawyers.

Vindictive? Maybe. Angry? Yes. Justified? No doubt.

The plane landed in Texas and Michael reassessed. He had not read but a few words of the book he held in his hands, *The Notebook*. It would soon be time for him to look up his old college friend Pablo Martinez.

He thought about Pablo as he gathered up his luggage and had it packed off to a taxi. He rolled off a $20.00 tip and had a nice time trying to speak to the driver in broken Spanish. His Spanish (he had had three years of it in college) came back to him easily. He had a gift for language and liked to try. He found the name of his hotel in his shirt pocket. La Quinta on Palm Avenue. The heavily burdened cab took off with an exhaust fart and Michael found himself grinning inside and out.

Pablo — what a guy. He would probably be surprised to hear from him. The little Mexican was five foot seven and weighed 170 pounds of pure, sinewy muscle when he had last seem him two years ago at a meeting in Albuquerque. He was also fifty and single since his wife had died of ovarian cancer a few years earlier. In McAllen, he was surrounded by his siblings — four brothers and three sisters. The brothers were older, and his sisters younger. His brothers, he knew, ran the family grocery store while one sister was a housewife, another a successful real estate executive in Tucson and his younger sister was getting a Ph.D. in anthropology at the University of New Mexico. Michael had seen pictures of them all, but the picture of Rosa, the younger one, was fixed in his mind. She was pretty and, he knew, very smart.

Pablo was a G.P. and a good doctor. He had many interests and took the time to pursue them. He was an outstanding horseman who liked to play western polo and was proud of his string of half-Arabian/half-mustang horses that he carefully bred. He climbed mountains, he sailed, but most of all, he liked to explore horseback, muleback, and on foot in the back country behind the Sonoran Desert. He collected Indian artifacts of many kinds. He stored some of them lovingly in a specially built case at home, but gave many more to museums in Mexico and Texas. He loved to sing, dance and play guitar with the mariachi bands with Spanish trumpets blaring. He was a fine fellow most of the time but sometimes seemed abrupt and rude with no time for anyone. He seemed to be constantly moving and avoided eye contact. In short, not everyone liked him, but Michael did and for some reason the opposites became best friends during school.

One year before all this, they met at a medical meeting in Santa Fe. This was not planned. They had a grand time drinking beer and going to sports bars to play pool, watch baseball and flirt with waitresses. One night before closing, Pablo told Michael an interesting tale. While exploring caves and climbing rocks in a desolate part of old Mexico, Pablo had come across a dinosaur graveyard. Preserved bones, bleached white by the sun, lay scattered on the ground only partially covered with dirt. Back bones, the vertebrae of the ancient animals, protruded from the ground. Something had caused all these bones to calcify and were preserved forever like stones. He knew that there were many small caves in the hills that contained artifacts, small statues, flint arrowheads, stone knives and small utensils of obsidian which must have come from thousands of miles north. Pablo's theory was that these things were brought with them as the Indians passed through going who knows where. Small objects that resembled buttons with holes were found inside some of the small statues. They were made of jade. Of course, there was lots of turquoise. After telling these things, the Mexican became silent.

"If you come down to see me," he said after awhile, "Don't tell anyone at all, you hear?" He brought out a pen and card from a motel in McAllen. On the back he deliberately wrote a telephone number. "This is my very private cell phone," he said. "Show it to no one, not even your wife." He paused again for a moment. "It is very — OK — secret — uh — private. *Sabe*?"

The entire subject was dropped and the friends parted without speaking of it again.

Now, here was Michael in McAllen, Texas under pretty strange circumstances himself. After checking into the relatively modest hotel, Michael collapsed on the bed and slept ten hours straight. When he did wake up, it was in the morning. He was still in his clothes. He felt groggy, like he had a hangover. After showering and taking a couple of aspirins he felt much better. Hauntingly, he thought of Patricia. He wondered where she was and what she was doing. He wondered and he ached and he missed her.

After a large breakfast of eggs and sausage, Mexican style, and a few cups of strong coffee, he contented himself reading the paper until eight o'clock, before returning to his room. He dug around in his address book, found Pablo's "secret" number and dialed him up.

"Leave your name and number," a voice not Pablo's said quickly. Michael did that and settled down to wait with, of all things, a Gideon Bible opened to Timothy. He didn't have to wait long.

"Hello, old Mike," Pablo's familiar voice came through. "How the hell are you anyhow? What are you doing here?"

"Hey, *hombre*. I came to see you and see those dinosaurs of yours," Michael said eagerly.

There was a long vacant pause before Pablo came back.

"Maybe, amigo. I have to arrange. Go see the town or whatever. I'll call you there at 8 o'clock sharp this evening. Be ready to move," he added. "I have a little trouble now." He didn't elaborate and Michael didn't ask.

"Huh? Well, all right. I'll be here."

"*Adios*," said Pablo and hung up.

Michael's day went by all right. He visited some western clothing stores, a book store and an art gallery. At 6 p.m. he had his dinner at the hotel and then went up to his room and packed. He felt rested, but anxious to be doing something.

At 8 p.m. the phone rang.

"Hey, Mike. You all packed up?"

"Yes. Where am I going?"

"Listen carefully but don't write it down nowhere. Go to the airport and buy a one-way ticket to San Antone. Don't ask questions, all right? I'll be getting in touch with you. Flight 731. Southwest at 9:30. Got it?"

"Yes, sure."

"*Hasta la vista.*"

Michael checked out paying with cash, caught a cab with all his stuff and headed for the airport. He bought his ticket as directed. When boarding was ordered, he presented his ticket to the counter and was given a red plastic card with the number 7 on it. The plane was a small turbo prop loading off the tarmac. Michael fell into the line and a red-faced Mexican stepped up to him.

"Michael, give me your boarding card. Thank you. Come, follow me." They passed by a man not quite in the line. The pass was given to this smiling hombre who entered the line in Michael's place. Michael was shown through a small door, down a passageway, and after three knocks a second door was opened that entered the terminal.

"Okay, señor. *Todo es bueno.* Go to the restroom, take a piss. Then go to the street outside the southwest baggage claim and wait on the sidewalk. Don't forget to wash your hands."

I don't know what is going on, thought the wide-eyed Anglo doctor. He shrugged his shoulders. *Who cares?* He did as ordered and waited patiently on the sidewalk smoking a cigarette (the first of the day). Soon a plain green, but new, Suburban pulled up, the back door was opened and Michael entered the back.

"Hey, old Mike. Good to see your shiny white face." He and Pablo exchanged a two handed hand-shake, followed by Mike getting a slap on the top of his head. That was one reason why some people didn't like him very well. It was a sign that Pablo was in charge and it established a kind of pecking order of sorts.

"Why all the intrigue, man? Don't get me wrong. I don't give a whit, kind of interesting."

"Then you don't have to know, do you?"

"Hey, Felix," he said to his driver. "Take us to a whorehouse." He looked at Michael with a wry charming grin. "Just kidding. Your dink would drop off around here. Felix is taking us to my night club."

"You have a night club?"

"*Sí, sí, señor.* Just got it a while ago. My apart-ment is upstairs and my games are downstairs. Well, actually, it's my brother Paul's. You like to play Craps?"

"Sure I do, if the dice aren't loaded."

"Hell, man, the house doesn't have to load the dice to win. Could be done though, but if we loaded the dice someone would squeal and we would be out of business in more ways than one. I forgot, how well do you speak Spanish?"

"I can read it pretty well but my español is *chis-toso* (funny). I have a dictionary. Are we going to old Mexico?"

Pablo looked very serious and became nervous.

"You are if you want. I can't quite yet. My sister Rosa will take you there. The college teacher, you know. Anthropology and sociology. She is tough as a mountain lion and smarter than a coyote. Watch out for her. She'll squish you down if you let her but then she will have no respect for you."

"My God, do you like her?"

"She is my *hermana*. I love her."

He lit a little black cigar and offered one to Michael. Michael took it with a grin.

"Two doctors smoking," he said to Pablo. "Are you still a sawbones or what?"

"Oh, yes, been only in Mexico. That's why I can't go with you right away. I have a clinic there in Mina. For poor people. I'll be delayed but I'll catch up when I can. I have some other — nasty — business that is kind of pressing. I have to visit with a guy named Oscar."

"Why are you hiding all this?"

"I am not hiding me!" he answered. "I am hiding you. Put it this way. There are some people who would really like to know where you are going and wouldn't want you to go there. *¿Entiendes?*"

"*Sí. Bastante dices*," Michael answered and shut up on the subject. "When do I leave?"

"It has to be tomorrow early," he answered.

Michael got the impression that Pablo didn't want him hanging around McAllen. For security reasons or what? He sure didn't know.

They had a drink of good tequila at the bar. Pablo informed him it cost $75 a fifth but it burned him just the same. He didn't know how to tell with or without the lime! Pablo hated Tequila. Felix showed him a nice, snug quarters where a lot of gear was laid out on the bed and in the chair. Cowboy boots that came up to his knees, riding breeches made of cotton twill, soft cotton flannel shirts, linen shirts, bandanas and a very nice straw sombrero with a chin strap. A belt was provided that had a buckle that looked like it was inlaid with green jade. Felix put them all in a bag that resembled a leather duffle bag, told him to pack his toiletries and underwear and socks. He left out an outfit for him to wear as well. Michael noticed it had been washed so it would be soft for riding and not new-stiff. He was a little surprised when Felix told him to hide his ten thousand dollars. *How the hell did he know? My God, do I sleep that soundly? Not usually.* Maybe that's why he felt so groggy when he woke up and needed aspirin, too. Then he remembered asking the skycap at the airport if he knew Pablo Martinez and he knew why the taxi ride took two hours instead of 45 minutes. The hiding place was ingenious. There were false sides and bottom to the duffel. He wondered what he was getting himself into, but he found more excitement and felt more alive than he had in a long while. He thought of Patricia only moments before he pushed her out of his mind and went to sleep.

Up at 4 a.m. with a gentle shaking and a welcome cup of coffee.

Felix smiling down at him looked like an old friend. Michael felt fine and rested this morning. He dressed quickly in his new duds and followed Felix down the stairs, through the night club hallway and out the door to the suburban. Felix handed him a plastic plate containing tamales and a plastic fork.

He washed them down with warm orange juice from a can and they were off to the nearby border crossing.

"Where are we going?" asked Michael.

"Across the border. First to the *clinica* for a day, then to the ranch of Homero," Felix replied. "Pablo's *Tio*."

Chapter 3

The border crossing went without incident. Felix knew the guard's name and the guard knew his. They smiled knowingly at each other as Michael presented his passport. He filled out a tourist card in minutes and they were on their way. They left, but Michael did not get his tourist card.

Soon they were in the heart of old Mexico going sixty down roads that should be driven fifty if that. When they turned west off the paved road onto the dirt road, it was still dark. The sun came up painting the desert around them with a myriad of various shades of red, orange and yellow. The hills in the distance that they were driving toward were a constant subtle blue-gray. They did not seem to be getting closer as they banged and bumped their way along. Sometimes they passed over and through creek beds, some dry, some actually running a small amount of water. At their place the mud was thick, gooey and sticky. It caked in the wheel beds, then dropped in chunks down the road.

The two men exchanged pleasantries in Spanish and English. Michael used his dictionary frequently, but pleased himself with how much Spanish he knew. Finally they stopped at the side of the road to drink a bottle of cold water from the ice chest, each a cold orange, have a quiet cigarette and take a pee.

"Lots to go, *vamos*," Felix said with patience, crushing out the butt of the cigarette in the dirt. "*Mucho lejos*."

"Hey, *hombre*, can you tell me where we are going?" Michael asked as they got in and took off again.

"To the foot of those mountains," he said nodding the direction with his chin. "About 40 or 50 miles as the road goes to the *clinica*."

Felix drove the Suburban in four-wheel drive. Over the bumps and rocks into the ruts, into the land that made the wheels spin and the engine whirl, across small streams that had only a trickle of muddy water and, now and then, completely off the road over the cholla to avoid an obstacle in the would-be road. Michael thought he had a dropped foot the way he kept the gas pedal down. The air conditioner didn't work too well. When Felix lit one of his black stogies Michael was forced to open the window until he was chewing on the dirt. If the big Mexican hombre knew he was torturing him, Michael never let on. Felix didn't make conversation but sang along continually to the merry Mexican music that screeched and scratched over the radio.

When they got to the *Clinica* Michael was most happy to get out of the car despite the heat and made his way through the dust to what he could tell was the front entrance. The clinic was a nice, almost new, doublewide trailer with an air conditioner that was choking in the heat and bouncing around like it wanted off the roof.

Michael looked at Felix. "Tighten that thing down." He was used to giving orders, you see.

Felix looked up at it, shook his head in agreement and returned to his car to get some tools.

Inside was pleasant, cool and clean. The receptionist smiled at them and called out to a nurse from inside the next room. A cute little fat Indian in green scrubs peered out at them.

"Say Doctor Michael."

"You're Doctor Michael?" she said in perfect English with no trace of an accent. "Doctor Pablo will be out directly."

Michael just stood around looking. The waiting room area had about twenty people sitting around. No one was reading anything. They were all just sitting, patiently waiting.

In just a few minutes Pablo came through the door, wearing scrubs and smiling for all he was worth.

"Michael, come in. Say hello to Sylvia and my little nurse Frances."

Everyone smiled, nodded their *cabezas* and said hello.

The back area contained three exam rooms, a toilet and storage area. Everything seemed to be made of stainless steel. Each room had a stainless steel cabinet that contained instruments, bandages, tape, syringes and needles, stethoscopes and thermometers. One room had disposable speculums and pap smear equipment. It was all neat, clean, shiny, efficient and professional. Pablo was obviously very proud, as he should have been. Across the hallway, past a small pharmacy, was a closed off operating room with lights, anesthesia machines, outside scrub

sinks controlled by the knees and first class operating tables, two of them. The walls were lined with
glass cabinets containing surgical packs and IV
equipment.

"You are ready to go!" Michael said with enthusiasm. "This is very well done."

"Thanks," was all Pablo answered.

"Let me ask you some questions if I may."

"Shoot."

"Electricity?"

"We have a top of the line generator run by a
combination of solar power and propane."

"Water?"

"It was a problem. I sank a 1000-foot well before
I hit enough good water. Now we have plenty and
the Indians come around to fill up their barrels and
jugs.

"We are getting more solar equipment," he
added. "Eventually the A.C. will be safer."

"Tell me about your patients," Michael said
respectfully.

"These people are Indio Indians. They speak
their own language and most of them can't speak
Spanish. They have never been to school. They were
completely neglected, still are, by the Mexican government. They had virtually zero medical care until I
opened this place."

"Do you get paid?"

"I do not ask for pay. The government pays me
pennies. The Indians, that's the story, pay me if they
want to. Some do. Some don't. This has to do with

where you are going, up to the foothills." He led me into a small office area where we sat across from each other. I saw a small statue on the table made of coarse red clay. I recognized it at once as being a pre-Columbian statuette. Big lips and eyes, with a fat squat body sitting cross-legged.

"The Indios," he continued, "began to bring me small gold nuggets, silver teardrops, pieces of jade, arrowheads of all kinds and some turquoise as well. What was really fascinating were the needles and pins made of ivory."

"My God, that's interesting."

"Everyone around here was sworn to secrecy, but word got out. Now I am having a little problem with a *cavrone* named Oscar Gusman and his gang of thieves. He is a powerful crook with a lot of connections. He is coming down soon.

Michael didn't ask what he meant by that.

"The stinking corrupt government hasn't learned about things yet. I suppose they will. I want to be ready. They will take everything and stamp the Indians into the dust."

Just then an Indian lady walked past the door and gave us a smile. Pablo stood and said hello and some other things Michael didn't understand.

"That woman saved me."

"Oh."

"My mother was from around Mina. She didn't have milk for me and she, Cresa, nursed me for a year. What a story, huh? Needless to say, I take good care of her."

"You said you would do a few operations," Pablo said suddenly, changing the subject.

"I did?"

"You said you would help."

Michael paused long enough for proper dramatic effect. "Of course I will."

Pablo led him to the restroom area that doubled as a dressing room. Michael put on scrubs and walked to the operating room. On the operating table a three year-old boy lay quietly. Michael saw at a glance that the boy had a large umbilical hernia pushing his belly button out like a beer bottle.

"Pretty big."

"Can you do it?"

"What do you mean, 'Can I do it'? Of course I can do it. Do you have any <u>Morlex</u> mesh?"

"As a matter of fact, we do. I brought it especially for you. Go scrub; Frances is your scrub nurse. She's ready."

"I am always ready," said Frances with a naughty tone.

Pablo gave Demerol and Xanax through the IV, slowly, very slowly as he monitored the blood pressure and breathing of the little guy as he snored blissfully under the facemask. I used Lidocaine 2% mixed half and half with Marcaine 5% to make a good regional block. I reduced the hernia into the abdomen after dissecting it free from the apex. Luckily, it went in easily and I didn't have to open the peritoneum. I folded it inside. I cleaned the edges of the rectus sheath, folded a square of <u>Morlex</u> and sewed the rectus sheet over it. I trimmed the excess skin off and closed the incision with the skin clips that Frances provided. The boy began to stir with the last clip. I felt good. It had gone well. I felt like the good surgeon I knew I was. Funny, I couldn't help thinking that the first surgery I ever did solo was an umbilical hernia that bled inside and I had to go back and repair. I felt like quitting right then.

After a lunch of cold beans and soft tacos made with goat meat washed down with water, Pablo presented me with other children with inguinal as well as umbilical hernias. We repaired them all without a problem. He brought in a man, about forty, with both his arms in splints. We saw him in one of the examining rooms that had an X-ray screen. Pablo held the X-ray up to the light. Both of his ulnas were broken. The bones were bent, fractured clear through and were touching the radius.

"My God, who did this? They must have used a crowbar. These are nightstick fractures."

People get nightstick fractures when they hold their arms up in front of their face to keep from getting hit by the policeman nightsticks.

"You're right. He used a fucking crowbar. Wait 'til you see what he did to his daughter."

"Who did it?"

"Oscar's man," was all he answered.

"Why don't you call the police?"

"Are you kidding? The police wouldn't even come to see an injured Indian. This is Mexico, remember?"

Pablo's disgust for Mexican justice was apparent. He brought in a girl of twelve years with a gash in her upper lip that was an inch long. The girl was tearful and quiet as Michael examined her.

"Her lip is split clear through. Her teeth are loose but look all right."

He pushed them back farther into their sockets. Three front teeth on the left side.

"When did this happen?" asked Michael.

"Same time as her father's arms, about ten days ago."

"What happened, for Christ's sake?"

"Oscar found out this guy gave me some gold nuggets. I am not sure how he did, but I'll find out. He sent his man to get it out of the old man where the Indios had been getting the nuggets. Hell, he didn't even know. His father or grandfather found them years ago and they have been in a pot in his house. The Indios have been very careful to keep their secret. Most of them have a few hidden away. They don't know where they came from. I think they don't know. At least they won't tell me. And they trust me," he added. "As they should."

"Let's do the little girl first," said Michael.

Pablo brought her into the O.R., gave her a little sedation and prepped and draped her mouth. Michael made the whole lip numb with xylocaine with epinephrine. He used acrylic dental glue to hold the loose teeth buttressed to the solid teeth. Michael used magnifying lenses to approximate the vermilion border. The skin was closed using very fine nylon sutures, taking great care to trim away any ragged edges. The inside of the lip was closed with suture material known as Monocryl that took weeks to absorb. It caused no internal scarring at all.

Michael looked at his work and smiled. Frances and Pablo expressed their pleasure with praise that was not entirely spoken. Michael felt good. Doing something well is its own reward, whether it's painting a picture, singing a song or repairing a little girl's lip. *Gratitude is one thing that should never be expected*, he thought.

Next, they brought the man in. The splints were removed and both arms scrubbed thoroughly and painted with Betadine iodine. Carefully feeling the ulnar bone, threaded wires were drilled in above and below the fracture. In this way, the bones could be brought end to end and held there with a plaster cast being applied incorporating the wire. X-rays were taken which showed exact alignment.

Michael patted himself on the back psychologically while Pablo so did physically.

Michael explained, "The ulna can't touch the radius at the fracture sight or the two bones of the forearm will grow together. Then a guy wouldn't be able to turn his palm up or down. He will need to be in plaster for six weeks. He will have permanent knobs on each side, but the bones will be stronger than ever in the long run."

"Hey Pablo, what happened to the bad guy?" asked Michael.

"I'll tell you, then you forget, okay?"

"Sure."

Pablo walked Michael out into the waiting area where a boy of thirteen sat patiently waiting. "Meet Louis."

"Hello, Louis."

"Louis shot the son of a bitch right between the eyes with his .22 rifle. They sent for me and I beat it out there. We loaded the guy in his Jeep and then I drove him to an old deserted mineshaft. I parked the Jeep inside with him in it, then we took dynamite and blew the entrance shut. You ever use dynamite?"

"No."

"Well, I'll tell you three sticks is an awful lot! We almost blew the mountain up. Two thousand years from now some archaeologist will dig up the Jeep and will write a bunch of papers about how aliens came up from the center of the earth or something. Anyhow, that's it. Let's go *comer*."

A large travel trailer was parked near the clinic where Pablo and his two nurses stayed. Any patients or families were on their own. Some patients were kept in the infirmary overnight, but not often and none were tonight.

* * * * * *

Michael, Frances, Sylvia and Pablo had a nice roasted chicken dinner with three bottles of Almo white wine. Michael flatly refused any tequila despite Pablo's urging.

"The stuff is fifty dollars in Mexico," explained Pablo.

"Put it in your cigarette lighter."

"I can't. I am afraid it would blow my hand off."

Exhausted, Michael crawled into the bed Pablo provided for him. The air conditioner was noisy, but he was comfortable. He had just fallen asleep when incredibly smooth legs next to his woke him up. Frances was there with a beaming smile he could just barely see in the dim light. She wore only a scrub shirt.

"I brought you something, Gringo Doctor."

"Frances, you brought me something? What did you bring me?" I asked.

"A gift from Pablo."

"A gift from Pablo? What?"

"A Mexican blow job."

With that she undid the tie from his scrub pants and pulled them off with little tugs at his ankles. Michael didn't know what to say so he didn't say anything. Frances rubbed her hands together, then spread creamy aftershave lotion slowly on his scrotum.

"I always liked Mennon Aftershave Lotion," he whispered. She was gone for a minute and then, after a while, she returned with a mouthful of ice cubes. She opened her mouth and took him in slowly, gently and repeatedly with gentle suction and a massaging tongue.

"I think I am going to faint," gasped Michael.

"Not yet," mumbled Frances with her mouth full.

When the eruption came, Frances barely got out of the way. The ice cubes went flying and sticky stuff lit in her hair.

"You must have been storing that up for a while."

"Uh…" mumbled Michael.

"Are you happy?"

"Uh-huh, but I want to be inside you."

"No way. I am Pablo's woman and I am faithful."

She got up and left the bed. In two minutes Michael was fast asleep.

In the morning, he awoke to the smell of sausage, eggs and onions frying along with some sliced green peppers. He found his pants on the floor and pulled them on over his still semi-erect penis. It felt like a greased summer sausage.

Everyone ate breakfast and drank coffee while they chatted about the sun, dust and cacti.

Felix and his Suburban appeared out of nowhere and after handshakes and cheek-kissing Michael was on his way again. Boy, he didn't feel bad at all.

"Where are we headed now, *hombre*?" Michael asked

"Over there," said Felix, pointing to the blue hills in the distance. He lit one of his foul cigars and blew blue smoke at the windshield.

"What is there?"

"That's one of Pablo's little ranchos. His uncle lives there and runs the rancho. His sister, Rosa, is there with the mules and some guys who work for him. I mean his uncle, Hamero."

"Sister Rosa? Pablo's sister Rosa?"

"Sí, *es verdad*. She is there."

Felix's expression and tone gave away nothing really, but the way he said "She is there," revealed respect. Maybe something else. The picture he had seen of her was when she was only 18 or 19. She, of course, would be in her early thirties now. The doc was glad he had pawned his wedding ring and sub-consciously felt his ring finger.

"Is she single, Felix?" Michael asked as casually as he could.

"I think so," was his only answer. They bounced along too fast over the road which never seemed to be straight for long for some reason. Felix told him it was the way the stagecoach had gone in the past to avoid the side hills and little gullies that were hard not only on the riders but the horses and coach as well. Felix made exaggerated humps up and down like he was riding on an old stagecoach with leather straps for shock absorbers. He didn't have to exaggerate much with the tough old suburban ride.

When they came to the rancho, nestled in a small canyon between rocks with oak trees planted all around the house and an acre-sized yard, Michael was pleased to see green grass as well. The ample sized ranch house had been recently restored judging by the new paint and a board walk leading up to the porch that surrounded the house that looked unused.

People were waiting patiently as they walked up to the porch steps. Three men, an older one dressed in clean clothes and two apparent cowboys with broad sombreros and high-healed boots with spurs. Their clothes were not particularly clean.

Introductions went around in Spanish. Only the older man came forward to shake hands. The cowboys nodded their heads in Michael's direction and lifted their hands waist high in a polite wave. The cowboys were Luis and Rudolfo. The distinguished older man was Homero. Homero proved to be Pablo's older brother who lived in Mina. He was the overseer of this ranch as well as another one 30 miles further into the hills. He explained that he managed Pablo's "other interests" in old Mexico. The man was charming. He was friendly and considerate of Michael's stumbling Spanish and proclaimed that his English wasn't much better. (He was being polite; his English was fluent.) Homero and Michael sat on the veranda smiling and talking with short sentences to each other, while Felix left toward the barn and corral area visible from the porch.

Presently, Michael heard female voices, the screen behind the door opened and two women appeared carrying a pitcher and glasses on a tray.

The older one, obviously Homero's wife came forward to be introduced. She was round-faced, plump and happy looking.

"Nice to meet Pablo's old friends," she said in broken English. "He speaks good things about you.

He is so busy. He doesn't have many friends. *Mi casa es su casa.*"

"*Gracias, Señora. Muy amable.*"

Then Michael got a look at the young woman with her. It was Rosa and she didn't seem particularly impressed that Michael, Dr. Hart, M.D., Fellow of the American College of Surgeons was visiting his presence on them. She looked a little annoyed.

Michael spoke first and made a point of putting out his hand for a shake.

"You are Rosa. I saw your picture when your were eighteen getting out of high school. Pablo was very proud of you and showed your picture all around. You were cute then, but you are beautiful now."

She took his hand for a shake in a business-like fashion. Her eyes did not avoid his but she seemed to be looking through him.

"Thank you for the compliment, Dr. Hart. Sit down. Have some rum and lemonade." She motioned him to a soft chair and put a glass in his hand. It was stuffed full of ice cubes, cold snappy and good.

"Ice! You must have a good source of electricity."

The comment was toward Homero, but Rosa answered.

"We have solar panels that run our air conditioning as well as our generator. The generator has gas as well that keeps the battery up. Mexico is well ahead of the States in solar energy, particularly the kind that is augmented by fuel."

"Like a hybrid car, Toyota," he said knowingly and approvingly.

"We make Volkswagens in Mexico."

Michael felt put down by her and he was confused by her demeanor.

There was an uncomfortable silence for a few minutes.

"*La cena* will be ready soon, Dr. Hart," said the Señora very politely. "Rosa will you show you to your room so you can wash himself... or..." she left it hanging. Everyone but Rosa smiled. Rosa rolled her eyes.

"Come on, Dr. Hart. Bring your drink." She proceeded inside, barely looking back for him.

"Excuse me then, good people," said Michael with a little bow, then followed inside.

Rosa showed him a very small but quite cool room at the back of the house. The room had an adjacent bathroom painted a shiny white. There were pictures of Mexican cowboys in all kinds of poses painted directly on the walls.

Michael was enthralled by them. "Who painted these?" he asked Rosa. "They are very good. I know. I like to paint but I couldn't do these."

Rosa seemed to melt a little. She smiled showing her beautiful white teeth outlined by full lips with just a hint of pink lipstick on them.

"Me. I painted those and all the others you will see around here. You like them, huh?"

"Yes, I do. Please show me the others around the house."

"All right," she said after a second's hesitation. "I will after we eat. After you are done washing yourself come down to the dining room at the end of the hall." She chuckled at her aunt's phrase, *washing yourself*. She was smiling again as she left him, closing the door behind her. Michael went over slowly and sat heavily on the bed. He took off his sombrero and ran his fingers through his shaggy hair. He thought about Patricia and how she didn't like his extra long hair cuts.

"Piss on her," he said to himself, reached over and drained the rum drink he had carried with him. Michael was in the habit of showering before bed. He went into the bathroom and looked at the shower. It hung on a plastic hose with a spray attachment on the end. "Perfect, all the comforts of home."

Dinner was a pleasant affair. They had grilled beef ribs smothered in salsa and smoked to perfection over a mesquite fire. Coleslaw, sliced tomatoes and wide slices of avocado marinated with onions in some sort of wine vinegar. Bread, like the best French restaurant. French fried sweet potatoes salted and peppered with mild chili pepper powder. Pieces of rubbery cheese like string cheese but much more tasty. All this and beer poured into frosted mugs from the freezer somewhere.

Michael made a big effort to smile at Rosa and catch her eyes. Sometimes he succeeded and he caught her smiling like a little girl back at him. He could not stop telling his hosts how much he enjoyed the food and thanked them for their hospitality.

Homero liked the fact that his wife was pleased by the compliments and attention.

After dinner was over and while the dishes were being cleared away, Homero suggested they step out on the porch and have a small Cuban cigar.

"I have a date with Rosa," he said politely, "but I would like a cigar."

Rosa looked at him and said, "I was going to show him the art work." She said it like a defensive explanation of the word 'date.' "I will come get you after the dishes are done."

"That's certainly fine with me," replied Michael as he followed Homero out the door. They lit their cigars. They sat contentedly for a while, then Homero looked at him seriously.

"I have a letter for you from Pablo. He wanted to be sure you read it before you started off. There is some danger," his voice trailed off. "He also wants me to give you a pistol. I'll give them to you later."

"Thank you, sir," Michael said a little bewildered.

"You will leave tomorrow, late afternoon after it cools down a little. There is a breeze that comes up in the evening. You will have to cross a desert so it is best to do it at night. On the other side, the boys will head north. Someone was stealing horses up there. You and Rosa will go south and west. Pay attention. Use your compass and make notes."

Michael started to say that he hadn't brought a compass, but the man was ahead of him.

"I will give you a special compass with a range finder. Like I say, take notes. Rosa knows the way, but you will not survive if you get lost by yourself."

Michael nodded assuredly.

"There will be a major surprise up there," he laughed pleasantly.

"What?"

"If I told you, it wouldn't be a surprise, but for one thing there is a nice little cabin there with pretty good water. Not far from the bones and right with the caves around you." His eyes literally shined. "I wish I was going with you, but" he waved his hand in the air. "Business and cattle things." No one said anything then. "Rosa is tough. She will take care of you. Whatever you do, listen to her and do exactly as she says."

The two men finished their cigars peacefully watching the sun go down over the blue mountains. A red glow filled the sky and continued for a long time. The last plaintive bird songs died out and the night sounds took over. Off in the hills, coyotes began their yodeling calls to each other and to the moon. To them, they were singing their opera. Once he asked an old cowboy why coyotes howl and sing.

"Well, boy, that's because they can," was his jovial answer. People do things because they can. He used to think that, like monkeys that do things simply because they do it well, people do things because they do it well. Not true for people exclusively. They do things because they wish they could do it well lots of times. He played golf poorly and never got better, his wife stuck with tennis although she didn't like getting all sweaty just to get beaten every time. He bought a banjo and pounded relentlessly on the piano, both of which only gave him pleasure and did nothing for anyone forced to listen. Michael liked to sing because he knew he did that well, especially in the shower where the acoustics were better. Michael found himself chuckling at that thought, saluted the coyotes, said his leave to Homero and passed into the house. He passed by Rosa in the hallway.

"Good night, *Señorita linda*. I am going to turn in."

"Good night," she said quietly as she passed him.

Michael undressed, took a nice shower, contemplated growing a beard and settled on a mustache instead, shaving all but his upper lip clean. He put on clean skivvies and slipped into bed.

Thoughts of Patricia screwing with Bob entered his head and would not go away until he went to sleep. He was troubled by something. He really didn't care about her. It was just such a humiliating insult to contemplate. An insult that made him mad. "Wait until she finds out she is broke and in debt up to her tits. I wish I could be there." No he didn't. He was sad. He didn't have any more cigarettes. Good time to quit.

Chapter 4

Michael slept hard. He was vaguely aware that he had been dreaming. Something about a bucking horse that he couldn't control. His morning erection actually woke him up, but he was aware of the bustle in the house and voices speaking rapid Spanish. He glanced at his watch and sat upright. My God, it was 9 AM! After a long piss his penis returned to normal so he got dressed rapidly and went into the dining area. Food was being set out: bowls of fruit, orange juice, coffee and the ever-present breakfast tamales. Michael was hungry and after the thank you and good mornings in Spanish and English he ate with relish. He tried small talk with Rosa, but she looked grumpy and the conversation went nowhere.

After eating they finished the rich, dark coffee.

"Can we see your artwork now?" Michael asked.

"All right," Rosa said getting out of her seat.

"I have work to do in the barn," Homero stated.

"I will come along and help if I can," Michael said eagerly.

"After you see the art," Rosa said.

Everyone laughed a little at her tone.

On the walls throughout the house pictures were hung carefully balanced for effect and continuity. All at eye level for his six-foot frame. They were good. Full of colors that were bright and cheerful. Red, yellow, orange, blue, green, subtle peach and pale lavender were blended together in each one that created beauty of its own.

"These are so beautiful," exclaimed Michael. "Why don't you sell them?"

"No one wants to buy water colors. Mexico is full of people who do water colors."

"But these are good. I know a little about art. These are really sensitive and so pretty."

"I wish the world really was that pretty," Rosa said almost to herself.

"Rosa, don't you know that through your eyes it is. The world is this pretty. Beauty goes into your eyes, to your brain and heart, then out your brush. In a way you are a creator, in another way a recorder. But anyway, an artist with all that that means. What a gift. You do it because you do it well," he added very quietly.

"What?"

"Never mind. Just more praise. Can we see your workshop? I know you make pottery things too."

"How do you know?"

"Rosa, you couldn't help it."

They went to the back of the house where a room, bright with large windows and a skylight, contained a potter's wheel, a kiln in the corner, and buckets of various colors of clay. On the bench were finished articles that were waiting to be put in the oven. Several more were sitting on the floor that were fired and completed. Michael studied the shapes. Round, melon-like, gourd-like with curved handles, plain round handles on flowerpots, curved handles on water jugs and bowls with lids. Pots that looked like old-fashioned chamber pots and pieces that looked like large soup bowls. Cups with funny handles, heavy and thick. The colors and designs were original and unique to each one. Some contained sun faces, others, deer heads, flowers, trees, horses and burros.

"Did you create all of these?" He was glad for using create instead of made.

"The colors, I have never seen anything like it.

"These are natural colors mostly, but just store bought acrylics for the bright ones. No I didn't make all of these. I made very few of them. My mother when she is here, but mostly mi tía. You really like them don't you? You are into color I think."

"That's true, but the designs." He picked up a plain red clay statuette of an obvious pregnant woman with big lips sagging breasts. "Where did you get this it? It looks very old."

"You will find out, *gringo*."

She continued opening a big, heavy drawer that was on rollers. Michael stared. It was filled with gold nuggets the size of large peas, buttons of silver the same size. Rounded, green objects that were jade. Some shiny buttons and various sized pieces of turquoise, all of which had creases of minerals in them.

'Where did you get all these?" What are you going to do with them?"

"Hey, *gringo*, you will see where they come from if you are lucky." She closed the heavy drawer on the rollers. "When I get enough I am going to make jewelry."

"Seems to me you have enough."

"Not quite. There are some things I am looking for, garnets and ...." She let it drop.

Boy, there is something she isn't telling me, he thought.

"Let's go see the horses," she said to change the subject.

They met at the corral and barn. Several nice horses were milling around restlessly in the small enclosure.

Homero was cheerful as he stood there with a rope in his hand looking over the stock.

"Which one you like?" he asked proudly.

"All of them," Michael answered.

"Pick one," said Homero as he stepped to the corral fence.

"I like that big, black one with a white blaze there." He pointed to one standing alone in a corner.

"You pick a good one, *hombre*. He is very strong with a lot of spirit."

"That's what I like, *señor*."

"You can ride then?"

"Yes, I can ride."

"Do you want to try him out or wait until this evening?"

"It is hot. I will wait, but let me handle him."

Michael took a halter off the gate and approached the big, long-legged animal. The horse stood until he was four feet away, then bolted with a snort.

Michael followed him around the corral, being careful to avoid his rear end and front feet. He talked quietly to him but would not let him stop even for a second. The black began running around the corral with Michael just behind him. It took fifteen minutes or more until the horse, all sweated up and looking wide-eyed, stood still. Michael approached slowly, touched him on the neck and near the withers, then turned his back on him and took a step away. When the animal stood perfectly still he approached again, making noises with his lips. He touched him again, then reached to rub his chest. The animal moved away, but then slowly stopped again, looking at him. Michael ignored him and walked a short distance away, turning his back. He continued to whisper and rattle his lips quietly. The black took a step toward him, then came up closer, pushing his nose up against his shoulder.

"I'll be damned," said Homero. The other cowboys just watched quietly, saying nothing.

Michael reached around the horse's neck, then applied the halter easily with slow, deliberate motions.

"Let's be friends," he said. "*Amigos.*"

He led the horse away to the gate. One of the cowboys ran to open the gate and Michael went through with the black following like a dog. Michael began then to handle the animal all over. He rubbed his chest and his withers. He lifted each leg and massaged the muscles. He pulled his tail up and patted his rump. The black horse didn't move a muscle. The quivering had stopped. Michael took off his hat and patted him all over, rubbing here and there as he went over his body with his flapping hat. The trembling of the horse ended soon. Michael pulled black's head up to him and blew softly into his nostrils. The horse pulled back once or twice then stood there while Michael breathed into his nostrils. The animal allowed himself to be rubbed gently under the chin. Michael then turned his back and began to walk away. The big black followed behind like a doggy on a leash.

The cowboys were a little amazed, but Homero looked pleased by the show of horse *sabe*.

"You know horses, Doc," he said. "Let him put his nose under your arm. Here is an apple for him. See if he will take it from you."

Michael bit off a chunk and pushed it into the back of the horse's mouth. The surprised animal pulled back, tasted the chunk of apple and began to chew. He pushed his nose for more as the juice escaped his lips.

"I have a friend," said Michael with a smile. "The fucker is broke, isn't he?"

Homero laughed at him "Oh, yes, doctor, he is just a little particular who rides him."

"I don't think I will want any spurs."

Homero repeated that to the cowboys in Spanish. They grinned and laughed.

"You don't know," said Homero "all these ranch horses are ridden with spurs. It is how they are used."

"*Si, señor, ya entiendo*. We will see."

Rosa had been watching the whole scene and smiled appreciatively despite herself.

"*Venga aquì, cabarello*," they called to him. Michael came over to her standing by the gate.

"This is my horse," she said. "He was my horse, now you have him. I'll ride a meaner one that's faster. Can you ride?" she put in as an after thought.

"Hell, yes." Michael said back. "I was born on a horse. When I was born my mother was riding a pregnant mare with bandits chasing us. She got off, had me. The mare had its colt. She jumped back on the mare. I got on the colt and we got clear away from those *banditos*."

It took everyone a few seconds to digest it all. The cowboys did not need a translation by Michael's hand signals and expressions. They looked at each other approvingly and laughed.

One of the cowboys, Louis, took the halter rope and Michael followed Rosa out behind the barn where a small hill afforded a backstop. Homero came too. Some bottles and cans were already set up on the hill.

Rosa carried a Winchester model 94 30-30 carbine and a .22 Ruger pistol. She handed the pistol to Michael.

"I'm not much good with a pistol," Michael said with a shrug.

He fired a few rounds missing his target by two feet.

"If I may, Señor Doctor," brought forth Homero. "You are very steady, but you make mistake. Look only at the target not at the sights or the barrel of the pistol. Line them up in your — what you say — mind's eye."

Homero snapped off a shot and a bottle exploded. He did it again and again with the same result until the pistol was empty. He reloaded it again with 22 magnums and handed it back, handle first to Michael.

Carefully Michael did as he was told. It was very close. He fired again and a bottle broke. Again and another bottle broke. Four more times and a bottle broke each time.

"I'll be go to hell," said Michael to anyone who would hear.

"You are very steady."

"I am a surgeon, you know. We have steady hands."

"Bullshit," said Rosa. "You were just lucky." It was a kind comment filled with good-natured sarcasm.

"Let me see you shoot."

Rosa looked at him with half a smile, brought her rifle up and shot the little pieces of glass that were left all over the place.

"That was good, Rosa, but can you cook?"

"What?" said Rosa.

"Never mind."

Michael packed the compass with the built-in range finder, a tablet and pencils as well as his newly begotten pistol and ammunition in one side of his saddle bags while putting his shaving gear in the other along with packages of Handiwipes he used as toilet paper. He threw in his Spanish-English dictionary and a transistor radio, walkie-talkie combination with a range of 5 miles.

He waited for Homero to give him the letter from Pablo then in the early afternoon as the horses and mules were being packed he asked for it.

Homero made a bad show of playing like it had slipped his mind. Michael noticed that the envelope had been opened and clumsily resealed.

The note was short.

Amigo,

> *You are off on one hell of an adventure. I wish I could go with you, but business. You are under your sacred honor to keep the secrets of the place you go. Understood? There are people after me that I have to warn you about. They are a bunch of bandits and criminals but powerful in Mexico and the US border. If anything happens, do not come back this way. Go north directly to the border following the map I gave you. Follow the directions carefully. Use your compass and range finder to stay right on the trail. Carry as much water as you can and remember your horse will need some too. Go to the rancho marked on the map. There you will find my cousin Toney. Trust him, but not too much. Don't trust the two guys who work there. They have shifty eyes. He will get you across the border into the US. Get to the hotel in McAllen. I hope you don't mind the charade at the airport and now. Believe me. I am looking out for your ass.*

> *Take care. See you soon.*
> *Pablo*

What in hell? Michael wondered. *I wanted adventure, I guess I am getting it.*

He did not think of Patricia all day. He did wonder what his friends, associates and family would think. He told no one at all he was leaving, let alone where he was going.

After an early dinner of *Pallo Mallo*, rice and beans, all was ready. The pack animals were all in a row head to tail patiently waiting. Rosa was to ride a big heavy Palomino that acted a little nervous chomping at the bit. Michael's mount, the black Barbe, was all padded and fitted with a bosal around his muzzle instead of a bit. He looked dangerous but quiet. Horses like that often explode. Michael checked the girth making sure that the saddle was tight, then sprang aboard. He was ready. The horse bolted forward then reared up and Michael checked him with the bosal. The horse crow-hopped around in circles then started out in a fast trot in a zigzag in the direction he was used to going. Michael looked good in the saddle. He knew he did and he knew the boys, and Rosa, were watching.

"Easy," he said, "Easy, whoa, down." He touched the horse's neck as he pulled him into a jerky walk. He could see approval from the cowboys and nonchalant acceptance from Rosa.

"You should have given me that plow horse you're riding."

"He is not a plow horse. He is big and strong to rope cattle." With this she nudged the Palomino, who broke into a dead run. She ran him in a fifty-yard circle, returning with figure eights, in perfect control.

"That is a good horse," Michael exclaimed with appreciation. "How much do you want for him?"

"He is not for sale. You think you can buy anything?"

"I haven't got any place to keep him anyway." It was a friendly exchange that started the night-long ride off like a pleasant jaunt.

Michael kept careful track of the direction they were going. He tried to mark landmarks, but hell, there weren't any. Only rocks, cactus, mesquite and greasewood. He kept track of his position by the mountain off on the right side as they went.

Rosa, who was ahead of him came alongside. The horses who were used to going in a row didn't like the position well and fussed a little at first.

"Where did you learn horses, *gringo*?"

"I don't know why you are calling me *gringo*. Call me Mike. I think gringo maybe a subtle insult."

"In this instance, *gringo* is not an insult. It can be though. So all right *gringo*, I'll call you Mike. So Mike, how did you get good with horses?"

"Well, Rosey, if you must know, I spent my teenage years in a reformatory. You know, for bad kids. I really wasn't all that bad. I just stole cars, got in street fights, and burgled a few houses. Nothing real bad. I didn't kill anyone.

"Anyway, the reformatory they sent me to was a boys ranch they called it a boys ranch, but it was a reformatory in Oregon.

"Chasing cattle on half wild ranch ponies took care of whatever was wrong with me. I even got baptized and learned to say my prayers." This was told with a laugh, but he was serious. "I caught up with schoolwork and I found out I liked to study and learn. I even took correspondence courses in the winter when there wasn't much else to do."

"Like what?"

"Oh, literature was one, psychology, sociology, I don't know."

"How about your parents?"

"Well, my father was a merchant seaman. He was gone all the time. My mother had all she could do with eight kids. She went nuts. My big sister looked after me, but they couldn't control me much. I had a lot of rebelling in me. I was one angry guy."

"You are still angry."

"How do you know?"

"I know."

After a long lull in the conversation, Rosa said, "That is quite a story. You should be proud of all you have accomplished."

"Thank you. I had a lot of help. I am appreciative and grateful more than proud."

"I think you should be more proud, too."

Michael said nothing. They rode on through the moon bright night, stopping only for an occasional drink of water. Night hawks wing-whistled by and owls appeared out of nowhere to circle close overhead. A light pleasantly warm breeze touched their faces. Around them, coyotes sang to the moon and once they heard a rabbit's piercing squeak as a bob-cat caught him. Trees, bushes and bugs make some of the noises of the night. One has to listen with attention but you can hear even a bug hop from branch to branch if you do. Perched birds move from foot to foot. You can hear that, too. If you listen the plop, plop of horse's feet in the soft earth keeps time for the orchestra of the salient night noises like a met-ronome or a soft drumbeat can. Moon shadows are like ghosts when the shadow is from a giant saguaro cactus. The saguaros were spectacular here. They are 75 years old before they ever make a branch. They live in the most miserable hot climate in creation. During a rain, a cactus can suck up and hold a ton of water. The birds poke holes in them to live in and eat out the center without seeming to compromise the health of the plant. In the spring, in the right condi-tion, flowers appear on the tips of their arms, fol-lowed by fruit. People make jelly from the fruit. It is hideous. The cactus is squeezed out of its juice to make pulque beer and distilled down to tequila. The spirit, it is said, holds the blazing unforgiving heat of the sun. The mescal cactus, with its saber-like arms, have been eaten for centuries. A favorite food of the Apache. The base of the arms are like artichokes. They are soft after being baked in the ground for a day and very nutritious and vitamin rich. Peyote cac-tus, the size of golf balls, are dried and chewed alleg-edly for ceremonial purposes but now mostly for recreation trips without leaving home. The high is pleasant and a little known powerful aphrodisiac. It was heard that a man tried to fuck a pine tree. They would be something combined with Viagra.

Desert flowers are few and spaced far between. They don't last long as a rule. There are indentations here and there that retain enough water to allow them to grow. They smell sweet in the night breeze and in the morning light there are the purple sage of song and story. Under them, rabbits hide and like to make other rabbits. Rattlesnakes wait for small rodents and ground lizards to nourish their part in the scheme of things. Such patches are few. Men know they should be left alone (if only they would).

About midnight they came to the edge of the true desert of sand and rocks, devoid of plant growth for miles. Unbearably hot in the daytime and in the winter icy cold at night. There is no chill like desert nights in the winter. Now, however, the sands maintained the warmth of the day and the air was still. By the edge of the sand a trickle of water had been extracted from deep in the earth by a large windmill of remote timber. The trickle of precious water partially filled a watering trough. Each animal was brought up and each drank their fill before the trough was completely empty. They knew the trail and knew there would be no more water for a while. The cinches were checked while the animals were inspected for rubs. After a brief rest while the troop drank a bottle of water, they mounted up and were off again at a renewed pace.

It took four hours to trudge through the soft sand. The other southern ruin of desert sounds was marked by a strange margin of yellow grass that grew in small clumps. There they rested again. The animals were allowed to chomp some grass. They were tired. Michael's mount was as quiet as the rest. Michael blew softly in the horse's nostrils and the animal allowed it without protest.

"It is where we part company with our boys," said Rosa with a wave to the north. "We each have a pack mule with our gear on them. You take the ugly black bastard because it matches Diablo and I'll take the beautiful red one."

"Diablo. The horse's name is Diablo?"

"Yes," she snickered into her hand. "The mule is named Matador. Don't ever go behind him."

"*Matador* means killer."

"That's right, *gringo*."

"Now you tell me these things."

"You didn't ask. Let's go. We have a day ahead of us."

Michael and Rosa rode off each leading their respective mules. They simply waved a good-bye to the cowboys and their cows going in the opposite direction. They very half-heartedly waved back.

Chapter 5

It was five in the morning and the sun was just touching the western sky. There was no breeze. It was going to get hot soon. It was four hours to water and six hours to their destination. Michael was hungry but said nothing. Rosa must be hungry too. He saw her tighten her belt. *My God, her waist was slim already*. He tightened his belt as well. Later on, when it began to get hot, he saw Rosa unbutton all but the bottom button of her shirt and let the waist out. Michael did the same (*do exactly as she does*). The effect was to let the air circulate and when little intermittent puffs of breeze did come up, the shirts billowed for a little while anyway. Rosa was riding ahead, so it took a little while for him to get a look in her shirt. They were plump and smooth and pointed just right with natural roundness and pushed out nipples. *What am I doing*, he thought. God knows he'd seen lots of boobs. He had even manufactured a few dozen too. *But not Rosa's. Not until now.* He felt like a teenager and had to readjust his position in the saddle.

Michael had been careful to plot his map every mile or so or if the direction changed a little. The range finder was useless in estimating the distance to land marks. The range was about 500 yards. He figured out a way to judge things that were a third or a fourth away of the maximum then multiply 500 by the appropriate number. Not very accurate really, but better than nothing.

When they reached the four hour water, it was almost dry. Just a mud hole. They ran their animals back and forth through it (an old Indian trick to bring water up to the top). When water came up, the impatient animals drank their fill in 15 minute intervals. It was noon when they crawled back on with a couple of strips of jerky and another bottle of water in them. When they got off at the watering hole, Rosa buttoned up her shirt before getting off her horse. *Damn*, thought the *gringo*. She unbuttoned it again right away anyhow and dirty Mike got another good look. She caught him looking. She paid little attention.

"You have more hair on your chest than a monkey," she said not facing him.

"Well, what do you have on your chest?" he teased.

"I know what I have on my chest," she said.

"So do I."

"*Gringo travieso,*" she said wagging her finger at him like school teacher. Quickly Mike pulled out his dictionary. *Naughty! Naughty! She called him naughty!*

"I'll be dipped," Michael said out loud to himself.

They turned facing toward the low mountains ahead (Michael noted it on his map). After four hours more, the ground changed under them. There started to be clumps of the yellow green grass looking closer together. They passed an oak tree, then two. Ahead he could see some cottonwoods. *Takes water for cottonwoods*, he thought. They went over a little rise and then below them they could make out a cabin, a separate barn-like structure, a large round water tank, and a corral made of octo cactus surrounded the barn. It was a secure five foot fence. The animals walked in automatically then stood patiently, sighing.

The source of water was a small but clear creek coming off a hill in front of him. There was a flume made of rough boards that could be pushed into the flow to allow the water to go into the animals' water trough manufactured by rocks and the rock hard mud called calice that dries hard as concrete. By the time their trough was full and spilling out the top, Michael and Rosa had unsaddled and unharnessed their pack horses from their loads. He was a little surprised to see them all roll over before heading to the water. When the creek was allowed to flow freely from the flume, it filled many grooves cut into the corral floor for irrigation. The same method used for thousands of years by the Egyptians and the Mayan, Inca and Aztec Indians. The grass grew thickly, almost to the waist.

"They graze only an hour, then we put them in the barn or they will eat everything up in a day and trample the rest," said Rosa.

Rosa then went over to the flume. "Help me, *gringo*," she said, not expecting an answer. Together they pushed the flume over to the big round water tank made out of wood like a barrel. It was five feet deep and twelve feet in diameter. Small leaks appeared here and there. Michael supposed that when wood got wet, it would swell the cracks shut. He was only partially correct and some places were stuffed with wool cord hanging in the barn. It made excellent caulking. The tank began to fill but it would take awhile.

Michael carried most of the provisions into the cabin — all of the heavy ones. Rosa made several trips with lighter things. The saddles were brought up to the porch and slung over the rail that was built there for that purpose. Michael's shirt was left open. So was Rosa's. He took his shirt off and soaked it in the spilling water. He put it on again wet. Rosa looked and went over to the water spilling over the flume and did the same thing with her shirt. She kept her back to Michael as he made a big joke of trying to sneak around her.

"*Tonto*," she said as she buttoned halfway up.

The cabin was built against the rock face of the hill. A fireplace afforded cooking on a swinging arm and a flat grill. There was a crudely made plank table in the center of the room and four chairs.

On the wall, various utensils were hung. A couple of pans, pots, a Dutch oven, huge frying pan and a coffee pot.

"Just leave our stuff in the paniers," Rosa said. "We will take it out as we need it. Push them under the *cama*."

Michael noted there was only one bed with a rolled up sheepskin mattress over leather straps that went from side to side and end to end. It was a fair-sized bed all right, but only one.

"Are you rested, *gringo*?" asked Rosa.

"Why?"

"Do you want to go for a walk? You will see something I'll bet you've never heard of."

"Listen, as long as I don't have to ride anymore, it will be fine. My poor butt has so many blisters, I am tall in the saddle. How far anyway?"

"About a mile, but it is hot. So put the horses in the barn, will you? I need to put on something more comfortable," she said, like an actress.

Michael laughed at her as he did his chore. When he came back to the cabin, the young woman was busy putting some of the perishables in a sack. She wore khaki shorts like archeologists should wear with all the extra pockets, and tennis shoes.

Under the bed, Michael spotted a pair of sandals with thick leather straps and soles made of old tires. "These will be better than walking in those high heel cowboy boots," he said as he removed the boots and slipped his feet into the sandals. "They feel just right. Who left them here?"

"No one," said Rosa. "I brought them."

"Thank you. Now if I only had shorts rather than these jeans. Hey, I do," he said. He unbuckled his pants and quickly peeled out of them. He wore short boxer type underpants like the Navy issues, except they were blue and white. Rosa looked entirely unaffected.

"Do you happen to have a safety pin?" he asked. "I could use two…to prevent fallout," he said with a mock sincerity. Rosa just stood for a moment.

"As a matter of fact, I do." She rustled around in a pouch from her saddle bags and brought out two safety pins. "Do you want me to pin them on for you?"

"That would be nice."

"Do it yourself, *gringo*. Grab that bag and let's go."

Michael pinned the fly of his under shorts with the two pins, playing like he stuck himself.

"Do you have a Band-Aid to put on me?"

She didn't answer and headed out the door and off the porch.

Michael followed right behind her, soon sweating in the afternoon sun. He couldn't help looking at Rosa repeatedly. Her brown face was shiny with perspiration.

She is beautiful, he thought.

They walked down a faint trail until they came to a gash in the earth. It dropped down precariously for 100 feet. It was hard going. As the passage got narrower, he noticed there was soft thin mud on the ground and it was getting cooler. Odd. Farther down the passage ended with a slightly wider area. Rosa brought up a small camp shovel that had been left there and began scraping away a foot of loose dirt from the walls near the floor.

"Look," she said, stopping her work. "Feel."

He felt in the cavity that she had made. Ice crystals!

"I'll be damned," he said with amazement. "I never heard of such a thing. This ice must have been left here when the plates shifted over each other in the last ice age. For God's sake, 10 million-year-old ice. I knew there was a place like this in Oregon by the Dalles, but this! In the desert! This is something."

"You may not know it. We are at about 10,000 feet."

"No wonder I am short of breath."

"You get used to it in three days or so," she reassured him. "Look around a little and see what you can find."

Under a pile of dirt, Michael discovered beer bottles, the small old fashioned Mexican kind with faded warped labels, filled with beer.

"I'll be double damned. These have been here a long time."

"Yes, at least from the thirties when the cabin was built."

"Let's have one."

"Let's just split one for a taste. There aren't many."

"Well, we can leave them. I don't have an opener in my pockets anyway."

"You don't have any pockets."

"That's part of my point." He put the bottles back and carefully covered them. Rosa dug out a bigger hole where there were lots of crystals and put the bag of perishable groceries in.

"Our refrigerator," she pronounced. "I'm getting chilly. Let's go back into the sun."

"Yeah," said Michael. "My nipples are like frozen peas."

"*¡Tonto!* (which means idiot)" Michael chuckled to himself at the expression. The guy that wrote the Lone Ranger really pulled a good one. Indian companion *Tonto* meaning idiot and Tonto's name for the masked man, *Kemo Sabe*, meaning "know nothing." Great joke indeed.

When they were back at the cabin, they were both perspiring profusely. Michael was a little out of breath but Rosa wasn't at all.

"Let's check our swimming pool," she said as she peered over the edge. It was almost full of water. Michael put his hand in and splashed Rosa. He was pleased how cool the water was. "Must be ice where the water comes from," he surmised. He scrambled up the rock above the pool that was on the side opposite the cabin, kicked off his sandals and jumped in with a yell and a splash.

"Man, this is unbelievably nice!"

"Wait for me," laughed Rosa. She went into the cabin and reappeared carrying a bottle of shampoo and wearing a large T-shirt with a V-neck that stopped at knee length. She too scrambled up on the rock by the small steps that were cut there, kicked off her shoes and jumped in with a shriek. Her T-shirt went right up over her face. She clutched furiously to pull it down while Michael laughed heartily.

"That was cute," he said.

"*¡Tonto!*"

She shared the shampoo with him and jovially lathered up, ducking under several times to rinse off.

"This is the best damn bath I ever had," exclaimed the wet-haired comic.

"Don't look when I climb out of here, gringo," she warned.

"I won't," he lied.

She stepped up a little ladder but had to reach high for the last step. Up came her shirt and up came a part of Michael that he wasn't expecting.

"Are you coming out of there?"

Michael looked up and smiled. "I'm afraid I can't come out just now."

She looked at him with understanding.

"Pervert."

Rosa left her T-shirt on. It clung to her, beautifully draping her pointed breasts. Another, shorter pair of red shorts she slipped under her shirt.

When Michael emerged from the pool almost under control, but not quite, he found a small fire made with mesquite chips. The frying pan and another small pot were over it on the grill. Soon the cabin was filled with the smell of onions and beans in the pot. When the frying pan was hot, two large rib steaks seasoned with salt, pepper, garlic salt and a fine sprinkling of chili powder, were sent to sizzling in the pan.

"How do you like your steak, *gringo*?"

"Anything but raw or well done. I ain't that picky."

"You ain't, huh? Look what I got." She came up with a box of mountain burgundy from somewhere. He poured them each a glass.

"Here's to ice caves, ancient beer, swims at 10,000 feet and flying T-shirts," quipped Michael.

The look on Rosa's face was priceless. She started to speak but didn't know what to say, so sat down at the awkward table and ate. Steak, fried beans, tomatoes cut in slices and tortillas disappeared. It was getting dark when they finished the few dishes with water from the tank. Rosa lit two large candles and they went to sit on the porch. They sipped more wine and each gazed at the desert, wrapped in their own thoughts. Any thoughts of Patricia or surgery was pushed out of Michael's mind. It was really easy for him to do so. Finally Rosa spoke quietly.

"Are you married, Mike?"

"I am not married." It was a lie, technically, he guessed. But Michael didn't feel the subtle discomfort that boarders on guilt from lying. A half truth? A half truth is a whole lie really and usually more. More because there is an extra measure of deceit. At any rate, Michael was quite comfortable with his answer. "How about you, little sister?"

"I am not your sister."

"I am very glad of that."

There was silence for a comfortable period.

"I have sort of a fiancé." Rosa looked embarrassed.

"How do you have a 'sort of fiancé'?"

"I haven't told him for sure. There is no date."

"How long have you been 'sort of' engaged?"

"About four years."

"You're not engaged, Rosa. Love doesn't wait that well. Do you love him?"

A long awkward silence later. "I don't know" Rosa whispered.

"If you don't know if you love someone, then you just don't. Maybe you want to, but you just don't."

Rosa looked away. "Give me another glass." she said holding the mug out. Michael filled it and his own. He started to say something forgot what it was anyway or Rosa asked, "How do you know if you love someone?"

Michael sat down and stroked his chin like wise old men. *Me giving love advice?* he thought to himself. *Boy, that's ironic.*

"Well, girl," he hated his own fatherly tone, "Romantic love has indefinable attraction. It's true, physically and otherwise. The attraction can be based on beauty, sex or a whale of a lot of other things.

"Like what?"

"Well like need, acceptance, loneliness, social pressure to conform, pride of a trophy mate, envy of others, happy mothers." Michael stopped for a full minute. "But love like we are trying to get at, has something about it that I know, but is hard to express. It means that you want to be by them, with them, you want to share things about living with them, babies, maybe adventures, experience, companionship, jokes, but I think bottom line, a person is more concerned with the other's happiness more than their own."

"You sound like a shrink, gringo."

"Well, I read a lot of books, but I am afraid I haven't lived much of it. I always thought that unless I could be the best thing I could be in every way, I wouldn't be good for someone else. Respect I guess, self and otherwise."

"You always thought? What do you think now?"

"I don't know what I think. Trying to possess another is a big factor. That can't possibly work."

"Why not if they possess you too?"

Michael laughed. "Don't confuse me for Christ's sake. My mind is crystal clear!"

They laughed some more, drank some more. Michael, when he began to sing show tunes, he sang very well and he knew it, a beautiful lyric baritone voice that could reach to tenor range on some songs. Rosa listened to him, encouraged him, and she smiled and smiled. "I have become accustomed to your face." "The girl that I marry," "younger than springtime." "Until there was you."

Michael had a grand time singing those songs.

"You are a big soft romantic, you know that, Mike?"

"I am not. I am a tough cowboy."

They looked and talked about the stars. Finally there was a shooting star. Neither said anything for awhile.

Michael and Rosa sat sipping the red wine in a silence that seemed awkward to them both, that is until the wine warmed their inside like wine will do. Another shooting star streaked across the inky sky.

"You know what? When I was a teenager, when a guy was sitting with his girl and they saw a falling star, that meant he could kiss her."

"How quaint," she said sarcastically.

"I always thought that it should be some permission for them to kiss each other."

"Permission from who?"

"I don't know, but permission anyway for both, you know, to kiss each other. Who would want to kiss someone who didn't want to kiss them back anyway? You would kiss me back, wouldn't you?"

"Stay away from me, *gringo*," she said teasingly, squirming away from him on the bench in exaggerated fashion.

"Well, maybe if we were teenagers..."

"We're not."

"I know it. That is the only reason maybe I wish we were."

"What are you talking about?"

"Kissing because we see a falling star."

"You know you are kind of nuts?"

"Yes, I know it. But, God, I am a romantic nut. It is funny, but I thought that part of me was gone."

"What part, the nuts or the romance? What kind of funny, HaHa or peculiar?"

"A little of both."

"Don't be wishy washy."

"I haven't got a wishy washy bone in my body. I am just a tender, soft, emotionally charged, hopeless romantic."

"Well, I'm not."

"Yes, you are. I can tell underneath."

She had no reply.

"You know what, Rosa? The things be found, the statues and maybe even the dinosaur bones in some cases, they are the same age as the star. The shooting star is many light years away. I don't know what the speed of light is. I used to know, but I can't remember. Anyhow very fast, miles per second."

"186,000 miles per second."

"Smarty." Michael continued, "Anyway, when the star blew up it was 5,000 years ago and the light is just now reaching us on earth. About the same time the statues were made."

"How do you know?"

"You told me."

"I lied. They are between 1,000 and 2,000 years old, if that. I always exaggerate to make a point. It's more fun."

"That's not very scientific for an archeologist."

"Some things are not scientific," she said softly with a double meaning that hung in the air.

They felt warm and comfortable with each other now as they perused the sky for more dancing stars to shoot up the sky.

Rosa got up and went quietly into the cabin with Michael close behind. They rolled out the thick sheepskin over the strap bed together, not speaking. Michael blew out the candle and the room took on a yellow glow from the moonlight coming in the open door.

His arms found her waist and he pulled her gently to him. Her face turned up to his six foot height.

Her eyes were moist, almost crying, sparkling in the moonlight. Without speaking, his lips found hers. Warm, plump, soft and tenderly giving back his kiss.

"Oh, Mike." she whispered, "You are the prettiest *gringo* I ever saw. Make love to me."

On the soft sheepskin, his hands found the bottom of her shirt; she wiggled out of it and then out of her red shorts. Michael's hands and tongue and lips were all over her slowly but desperately. He loved her silky wetness, her taste, her smell, her hair, and her lips.

"I can't stop kissing you."

"I don't want you to stop."

So with a long kiss that couldn't stop itself on either of their parts, her legs opened a little wider and nature guided so well, he found his way inside her soft walls. Gentle, slow rhythmic, pauses, restarts, ending in gasping and whispered breaths and many deep kisses.

They held each other through the night, locked together sometimes, like spoons in a drawer. They slept soundly and peacefully until the sun came through the door to wake them up.

Rosa looked a trifle self conscious as she grabbed her clothes and headed out the door with out a single word. This morning's erection went away with his morning piss behind the cabin. He came around the big rock and climbed up on it to jump into the overflowing pool. Rosa was already in there splashing about.

"Did you pee in my pool?" Mike asked with mock sternness.

"Yes, I sure did."

"Good," said Mike and jumped in beside her. They kissed and held each other like they couldn't believe their good fortune.

Michael let the horses out to graze in the enclosure, then they had a cold tamale (of course) breakfast with mugs of hot coffee.

"I didn't bring you up here all the way to seduce you." Rosa said laughingly. "Let's go exploring. Just bring a couple of bottles of water."

"Do we walk?" he asked.

"Yes."

"Good."

"There was nothing wrong with you last night."

"That's because of all the wine you gave me. Forced me, actually."

"*Tonto!*"

They put the animals in the barn and trudged off in a southern direction. They came to a small field made bare by wind and sun. Michael looked and looked all about him. Bones. Dinosaur bones. Dinosaur back bones coming through cracks in the earth with their obvious spines pointing skyward.

Rosa, had never been here before. They were like excited teenagers, picking things up, brushing them off, then looking further. Rosa found a small petrified dinosaur egg. Unmistakable in its shape.

"I want to keep this." She said, and dropped it into her sack.

They spent a long time, looking, exploring, kicking at clumps of dirt and studying bleached white bones.

"How old, doctor?"

"I don't really know but at least 10 million years." was his answer.

"Amazing!" exclaimed Rosa.

'They drank a bottle of water. Rosa looked at a notebook sized piece of paper that appeared to be a crude map.

"This way," she said, "up into those side hills. At least they aren't very high."

"Rosa?"

"Yes?"

"Are there rattlesnakes up there?"

"I don't think so. Somewhere I read they don't live at 10,000 feet."

"I hope you're right," gasped Michael.

It was rough going but they hadn't gone 200 yards into the hills before they spotted the first cave. There were several, no more than six feet deep with openings about 2 feet square dug out at a time when the earth must have been softer. The first four caves had nothing in them other than pieces of broken pottery. The fifth one was behind a bush and would have been overlooked by casual explorers. Inside were three small statuettes made of red clay. They were really pretty, coarsely made and were not hollow but one piece of molded clay. The figures were all female with baggy breasts and enlarged abdomens of pregnancy, similar to the one Rosa had at Homero's ranch.

"Let's just leave them. They meant something to the Indians who left them here. They are prayer symbols asking for fertility. These are not Aztec or Mayan. Local Indians like the Anasazi did them.

"How can you tell?"

"I am an archeologist, you know. Let's go farther around the hill.

They made their way slowly and awkwardly over the loose and crumbly rocks until they were stopped by a shallow gorge that they literally had to climb and crawl into. They were rewarded by finding two adjacent caves. Inside the first was a treasure. On the ground were arrowheads, fine, half-inch size made of obsidian. And there were statues. Several. Some a foot high. These were different as well. Made and rubbed smooth by artistic hands two thousand years ago. The figures were three females and one obvious male with a large penis way out of proportion to his body. He had a leering smile engraved on his round face.

"Hey, looks like me," said Michael.

Rosa glanced at him without speaking. She lifted up a few of the best made arrowheads and put them in her canvas bag. "These are bird points. They are perfect. Absolutely perfect. Beautiful. You know that the obsidian has to come from at least 2,000 miles north of here? The native people migrating through here probably brought them with them. But there were trade routes, even then, that were quite extensive and more efficient than anyone could imagine."

"Migrating from where?"

"Well from Asia. You know, across the Bering shelf. It happened all right. The Athabascan Indians along the Bering sea speak a language understood by Navajo in Arizona and a tribe in British Columbia and Oregon."

She was animated and sounded fascinated by her own knowledge. The feeling was catching.

"I have read that when they arrived in the southwest there were other people here."

"That's right. The little cliff dwellers were here. The Ansazi. But you know what, there were regular sized people here, too. The San Joaquin man was 50,000 years ago. A jaw bone was dated by carbon 14. The find really turned a lot of things upside down. Other finds have documented previous people. Clovis points found in Washington state, Nevada and Texas are more like 10,000 years ago. Human foot prints have been found in Texas that could be 1 million years old."

"Hard to believe."

Rosa ignored him. "Here are some flint arrowheads. Later ones. How did they get here?" she asked herself. Then she picked up one of the foot high statues. She could hardly lift it from her position so shifted around so she could lay it with care on its side. An obvious clay plug was in the bottom, cracked and of different clay than the statue itself. The plug had not been fired with the rest of the piece. She produced a pocket knife with a leather punch and began working the plug out. When it was clear, she held the piece up, and bean-sized pieces of bright and dull yellow nuggets came out in a pile followed by flecks of dull silver and yellow-green jade and turquoise.

"My God," gasped Michael.

"Put this in your bag, Mike. All I want is the statue. It is very interesting. It isn't even Aztec. It is Mayan, I think. They opened others and found the same — gold nuggets, silver teardrops and pieces of jade and occasional silver nuggets. These things Michael put in his bag while Rosa selected the statues that interested her and left the others empty but in their places.

They looked in several caves that they found in the area. Many of the statues were hollow and empty, but many held the treasure as well. Mostly the larger ones that were shiny and well made. Rosa was business-like as she put the selected statues in her sack padded by dry grass. Michael noted that the woman looked a little more reserved in her enthusiasm than he would expect.

"Didn't you find what you were looking for, Rosa?"

"Yes and no," she answered, and they headed home with very little additional conversation.

"I noticed you didn't take the statue with the big pené," he teased.

"I prefer real ones," she shot back at him.

Chapter 6

When they returned to the cabin it was very hot with afternoon sun. They peeled off their clothes with abandon and jumped in the over flowing tank where they kissed each other, fondled and teased, splashing and laughing. That evening they drank more burgundy wine, ate a hastily prepared *cena* of beans and fried shredded meat with onions and tomatoes thrown in.

They sat on the porch for awhile contemplating the amazing day and listening to the night and watching for a shooting star and feeling the presence of each other. They made athletic love on the sheep-skin, desperate and quick with Rosa in command on top of him. Then as they fell back, love became gentle and caring with caresses and long kisses.

The early morning brought them to the trail. When they reached the dinosaur field Rosa paused and looked at the hills.

"I have an idea," she said.

"I will alert the media!" said Michael. "What idea?"

"Never mind. *Tonto, gringo.*"

She began walking around in a different direction than before. More to the south.

"Let's see what is on the other side of this hill. Okay?"

She didn't wait for an answer but trudged off ahead of him not looking back. By the time they reached the other side, they had each drank a bottle of water. Their shirts were opened and they were shiny with sweat. What they found startled them.

There on a wide flat shelf, were granite statue heads a foot or more around. they inspected them with awe.

"Look at these, Rosie! They have helmets with spikes on top. They have mustaches and slant eyes. My God, these are obviously Chinese. The Chinese visited Central Mexico 1000 years ago.

Rosa dropped her bag and sat panting on a rock. "Let's find a cave," she finally said. They went looking and found one under an over hanging rock that hid its entrance. Inside were well made and polished states of blue as well as red clay. Some were heavy and yielded gold and a few garnets. Others were quite empty. Rosa chose hers and Michael gathered up his treasure.

"Let's go further up the hill." Rose said leading on.

Fifty yards more they found rather large cave and explored inside. The statues were different still. Red and blue and some painted with yellow paint. There were penises and women in squatting positions with babies heads protruding from between the legs. Rosa took a good example of each. They were light. In the back of the cave, they located heavy ones. They were plain heads and bodies with feather scratched on them, painted in all varieties of earth tone colors.

"Michael," Rosa said holding one up. "These, these are Inca. Inca like from South America."

"Are you sure?"

"I'm sure."

Well if they could come from China, they could go to Easter Island, they could come here, I guess. But why?

"I haven't got the remotest clue." whispered Rosa.

Then they opened one that gave out its treasure almost reluctantly. Michael shook it gently. This was indeed different. The gold was shiny, not dull, balls some the size of marbles, balls, formed of purified gold. Not nuggets. Then out came some dull stones, opaque, like glass. Some very very lightly pink in color.

"These are diamonds, Mike."

"Well, I'll be."

"Unpolished diamonds. They are only found in South America, Brazil, and Venezuela. In Peru there is a diamond the size of a walnut with a hole in it, hanging around the neck of some priestess. Mike, there is no known way to make a hole in a diamond today. I just remembered," she added, "there is someplace in Arkansas where diamonds are found."

"Clinton wasn't one of them."

"What? You talk funny. *Tonto*," she added.

The diamonds, three of them went into Rosa's sack. They looked further around a dozen more coarse diamonds, and some pieces of polished jade that were perfectly square and had holes in the center. Those, along with a hand full of garnets, went into Rosa's sack as well with many other shiny gold marbles.

They found no more caves in the area, so satisfied with what they had, with a promise to return someday, they left, looking behind them and touching each other happily.

The next day, they slept later draped around each other's naked bodies. They teased each other up, and bathed a couple of times. Went out shooting the pistol and Rosa's .22 automatic rifle. Ran around naked in the sunshine, made love a lot, bathed some more, ate what they had left, drank all of the wine, then in the evening, packed their gear to go in the morning.

They fell asleep with the thought of the long trail out.

In the morning they ate cold beans and tamales and packed two apples each with trail mix.

The horses and mules were glad to be heading home. Michael looked at the map he had made and started out first. Rosa trotted past him. "I'll lead, *gringo*; you'll get us lost and we will die out here stuck together somewhere."

"What a way to go."

"*Tonto.*"

Down the trail, Michael saw a sudden flash off to one side in the distance. Like a shiny metal or a mirror in the sun. It was so unnatural that it caught his immediate attention. He looked through the monocular telescope part of his range finder compass. He was sure he saw a horseman disappear behind a rock.

"Rosie, did you see that?"

"Yes, we have company I think."

"They appear to be staying away from us."

"Just now maybe," Rosa said. "Load your pistol."

"It is loaded."

"Is it a .22 or a .22 magnum?"

".22 long."

"Change the cylinder to .22 magnum and load it up."

"As they trudged along Michael did as he was told, not questioning her. He kept the pistol in his lap."

"Oscar?" Michael asked.

Rosa was quite surprised.

"Oscar," she answered.

Michael kept vigilant watch through the day. Across an open field up ahead he saw a very large boulder and as he was looking at it through the scope, a flock of desert doves took off.

"They are not our friends, *gringo*. They want to kill us for what you have in your bag. They have been spying on us. I hope they didn't see us playing naked Indians."

"What should we do?"

The change in Rosa was remarkable. She looked hard and serious and commanding.

"We kill them first," she answered matter of factly.

"Angle off to the left and follow me so they can't see us if they are just watching the trail."

Michael followed her until she was about fifty yards from the big boulder. She got off her horse and motioned Michael to do the same. She was as calm as a gunnery sergeant. They tied the animals and began approaching the boulder from the opposite side from the trail. They jogged as quietly and as quickly as they could, bent over at the waist for no good reason.

They made it to the back side of the rock knowing they had not been detected. They went around quietly together. Rosa with her rifle-ready position and Michael with the pistol cocked and ready. Three men squatted with their rifles in their hands while the horses were ground-staked to the rear.

Rosa stood up. "Drop those rifles, *cavrones*," she yelled. They were startled out of their minds, but it became obvious in a partial instant that they had no intention of dropping anything and spun around in an attempt to fire. Rosa's gun spoke twice in a flash of time and two of the men went over with bullets in their brains. Michael had his pistol on a man who stumbled. When he came up Michael looked at his target and squeezed off. The man dropped his rifle as he fell over on his face with a bullet exactly in his heart.

Rosa walked forward rapidly with her rifle ready. There was no need — they were all as dead as the very rocks they were sprawled over. Rosa went to where the horses were staked and calmly spoke to them to settle them down.

"These are Homero's horses. Bring those rifles. They are brand new 30-30's."

Rosa was in charge as she put the rifle in the scabbard. She took the bridles off and tied them tightly to the horn by their rains. She just slipped them out of the rope halters they were staked with, then hollered and waved her arms until they ran off.

"They will find their way back to Homero," she said. "He takes good care of his horses."

Rosa wasn't even shaking. She didn't seem at all nervous. Michael, on the other hand, was a weak kneed, trembling lass.

Rosa looked at him. "I think I'm going to faint," she said quite unexpectedly as she slid to the ground.

Michael sat beside her and held her hand until they could both move again. They didn't even glance toward the bodies as they went back to their mounts.

They went off again. Michael found he was pleased that she let him lead.

It was evening when they came to the watering hole beside the sandy stretch of desolate desert. This time it had almost a foot of water in it. They let the horses and mules drink only in few minute increments so they wouldn't get a bellyache. There was grass that took the animals less than an hour to devour.

"Mike, you have a map from Pablo?"

"Yes. Right here. Are we going to his cousin's ranch on the border? What's his name?"

"Antonio."

"Yeah, Antonio. It must be eighteen hours from here."

"We are not going there, Mike. You are."

"What are you saying?"

"Mike, I have to take those findings into to Monterey to ship them to the museum of anthropology in Mexico City. Do you understand? I must, it is my duty."

"God, Rosa. I don't want to leave you."

"I'll be all right."

"That isn't what I mean. I want to be... be by you, be with you.

"I want to be with you, too."

"I could... Well, I could love you." Michael said taking off his hat. "I mean, really love you."

"I think you know, Mike, I could love you too." She put her arm around his shoulders and kissed the top of his head, bent low in defeat.

"Where are you going, *bandito*? When you leave Mexico?"

"I don't know. Can I come to Albuquerque where you are?"

"Yes, Mike. Forever."

They made love with tenderness on their saddle blankets. Michael noticed her eyes were overflowing and so were his. They made a plan for Michael to meet her at the university library in about 2 weeks. It seemed that there was one too many people in her apartment.

Never looking back, Rosa went across the desert sands and Michael followed his map to the north.

Chapter 7

It was pitch black and he was about to give up when he saw a dim light ahead. He checked his map carefully. It had to be Antonio's ranch. He worried about approaching it without getting shot. He rode up slowly and began shouting *'hola'* a fair distance away.

Finally someone shouted back. A suspicious man stood in the middle of the yard carrying a child's baseball bat.

"Buenos noches. Eres Antonio?"

"No Antonio fui ayer."

"Mi nombre es Michael. Pablo me manolo."

"Si? El gringo. El amigo de Pablo.

"Si. Es mi. Habla usted ingles?

"Some," he answered.

"Can we take care of my animals?" Michael asked before dismounting.

"Yes," the man said, coming forward to help.

That is the most shifty eyed son of a bitch I ever saw, he said to himself. *He looks like a rattle snake ready to strike. He was waiting for me like those bastards behind the rock.* Michael knew it by instinct and he wasn't wrong. After they unpacked and unsaddled. Michael kept close track of his leather duffle and his canvas sack. He noticed that the snake had picked up the club. Michael was ready when he came at him from behind. He turned swiftly, grabbed the man with his left hand, placing his right hand under his arm. He bent and threw him, all of this in one motion. Unlike the karate practice he was so used to and able at, he did not let go of the arm as he slung him over. He often wondered what it would be like. The arm popped like a broken limb. The man screamed and lay writhing on the ground.

Out of the dark shadow a familiar figure stepped out holding a pistol the size of an anvil.

"Pablo!"

"Hi, Mike."

"You were there all the time."

"I wouldn't let him hurt you. My god man, you were fast. I almost shot you by accident."

Pablo looked at the man moaning on the ground with a right arm that flopped crazily when he tried to move it.

"Gastone," Pablo said quietly. "I didn't think it was you, here working for that fucking Oscar. I would have sworn it was Paul. Sometimes I guess I can be wrong. Didn't I treat you great, Gastone? Didn't I take care of you? Didn't I watch out for your family? And you sell out to Oscar."

"Please!" was all that came from Gastone's lips before Pablo blew his head off with his 757 magnum.

"You know what, Michael? I still don't trust Paul. We have to be little cautious."

"Where is this Paul guy?" asked Michael.

"That's a good question. He appears to be talking on the radio." Pablo held up a hand-held RDF (radio direction finder). The transistor sized instrument stopped blinking its light. In a few minutes a blond haired, blue eyed dirty appearing man in jeans and a T-shirt with no sleeves came charging out of the house carrying a pistol. Pablo yelled at him to stop, exclaiming it was Pablo. The man approached cautiously. Even in the dark he looked shifty-eyed and ill at ease.

"Give me that damn pistol you idiot!" Pablo barked at him as he snatched from his hand. "I told you that you do not have any weapons until I give them to you."

"Why?" stammered Paul with his blond pony-tails flopping half way down his back.

"Because I say so. For one thing, if the *federales* catch you with it you'll never get out of jail." He changed his tone. "This is Michael Hart. He is the one I want safely across the river tonight."

Paul nodded but did not offer a salutation, let alone a handshake.

"Go get the canoe ready. I want him across before midnight. You have a bus to catch," he said, talking to Michael.

"Let's see what you have in the bag, hombre."

"Yeah, what an experience. Let me show you." Mike took the bag which weighed thirty pounds and spread a sample of the contents on a work bench. Pablo fingered them and looked pleased but not surprised at all. "At least thirty pounds of gold alone."

They brushed them back into the sack, made a show of lifting it and handed it over to Pablo.

"What are you doing?" Pablo asked with a grin.

"These are yours."

"Well you got them, man."

"Don't argue, amigo. I owe you."
Pablo just said. "You owe me nothing." But he held on to the sack.

"Here Pablo, take this bag."

Pablo took it, looking at Michael with clear respect.

"Thank you, Michael. It is a good thing you do. This all goes to the clinic and back to the Indians. It is a good thing you do."

There was a pause, long and open, and then Pablo spoke. "What are you running from, Michael? Can I ask as your *amigo*?"

"You can ask, *amigo*. I guess I am running from a lot of things, but mostly from a flat, disappointing marriage, betrayal, infidelity and things just gone wrong. I run from love to anger and hurt, if that makes sense."

"That makes sense, but it is always best to run toward something rather than away. When you run toward something you can, and must, leave something behind and take what you want with you. You must take what you want. Take what is valuable, that which makes you feel like yourself. What makes you like yourself; no, *love* yourself. Know that someday you can look back and see some good things, some good times. Then the pain will be gone. So, my *amigo*, be ready to look back when it is time and don't be afraid. Be two things: tough as hell and as kind and fair as the world will let you.

Michael looked pensively at the stores. "Like medicine and surgery," he said to himself."

"What?"

"Can I come back to the clinic and help out?

"You can live there if you want to."

"If I do, I'll end up taking Frances away from you."

"Not a chance, gringo. She told me that you have a cute little dink. Just like a real one, only smaller."

"You're bad!"

Again, they sat in silence, puffing on Cuban cigars.

"It sounds like you have thought about things a lot, Pablo. Are you religious?

"After my wife died, I thought about lots of things, I guess. A man must fight against the injustices of the world that can be fought, and then do his best to accept the rest. Some people must be shot between the eyes and others kissed on the cheeks."

Michael let that one go.

"About religion, Michael, I hate religiosity. Look at our heritage. The Spaniards gave the Aztecs a great choice 'Become Christian and be hung or don't become a Christian and be skinned alive.' Whole generations were branded and forced to live underground in mines their whole lives all for the hideous Catholic Church of the day. Little boys were castrated to sing soprano in the choir. Look at the Spanish Inquisition."

"That was a long time ago, Pablo."

"It goes on today. Priests molest little boys under the protection of the bishops in the United States. If this goes on in the United States of America where we wash our dirty linen for the world to see, then what the hell is happening in Europe and elsewhere in the world? The Church punished Galileo because he said the earth rotated around the sun. They locked him up. Now the president stabs science in the ass to protect embryos from stem cell research because it conflicts with his religiosity. The Protestants and Catholics are fighting in Ireland. Mormon offshoots have polygamy and child rape. In the name of religiosity, women are stoned and their genitals hacked off. They are killed for family honor and burned alive when their husbands die. All in the name of religiosity… Shall I go on?"

"No."

"I get carried away."

"You always did."

"I know it."

"Well, old Pablo, do you believe in God?" I asked my friend.

"Hell yes, and Jesus too. Do you think I am an atheist?"

"No, now get me across the river. But first I want to know something. When I got here, that dead guy paid a lot more attention to my duffel. Like he knew what was in it. He couldn't take his eyes off of it. That's what gave me the warning. Only certain people know about the money in there. Could it be that the one carrying the tale could be the same one who tipped Oscar's boys about the Indian gold nuggets?"

"That could be, all right."

"Felix."

"Yeah, Felix."

"Did you kill him?"

"No. I sent him away to Guatemala. I got him a job in a mine down there. Actually, it is a private prison."

"I would rather be dead."

"So would he."

"Hell, I owe you for the adventure by itself. There is one thing I would like to have out of there." Michael took the sack and felt for the deep corner and came up with a rough diamond the size of a lima bean.

"I would like to keep this one."

Pablo's eyes bulged. "Rosa has more. I would like to tell you what else we found. Granite head that are Chinese, pieces of jade. Arrowheads the more perfect and so sharp you cur your finger holding them, made out of obsidian for birds he added enthusiastically. And my God, man, a friggen ice cave in the desert. We ran into some bad dudes, Pablo. Little gun fight."

"I know about it. They were Oscar's men. They didn't know that Oscar was dead, but it probably wouldn't have changed their minds."

"This Oscar hombre, you say he is dead?"

"Yes, the poor son of a bitch died out in the desert. His car ran out of gas and he didn't have any water. Can you believe that? No radio or cell phone. My, my." He added with false regret.

"Funny, the guy was barefoot."

"Do you have the pistol we gave you, Mike?"

"Sure." Mike pulled it out of his big baggy pocket and handed it to Pablo. Pablo made a show of deftly spinning the cylinder. "One round shot."

Pablo brought a piece of pencil lead, like used for fishing weight out of his shirt pocket and crammed it down the whole length of the barrel. He twisted it off there then pushed it out of sight with a leather punch on his pocket knife.

He handed the gun back to Michael. "I just want you to give this to Paul. Tell him it's a gift for helping you or something."

Just then Paul approached up the trail from the river.

"All right, Pablo. It's about time you told me about fucking Oscar."

"Why do you have to know?"

"Listen I don't have to know anything except how to get out of here with my ass intact. He tried to kill me, *hombre*. That deserves me something so I'd like to know what is coming down and why."

"All right my friend," said Pablo quietly as they sat on a bale of bright green alfalfa. "Do you not smoke anymore?"

"No, I quit. Stop trying to change the subject."

"I do," said Pablo as he bit a small black cigarette and blew the pungent smoke from his nose. "Oscar. Oscar Gusman. May he not rest in peace."

Michael listened intently.

"I started a clinic for poor people about five years ago now. The people there were mostly Indians. Gespe Indians, forgotten by time and certainly forgotten by the Mexican government. They were

hostile and resentful for a time. Suspicious as hell.
Their bright eyed children, with the round faces and
bright teeth, were cute as angels. The men were
skinny and tired. Their women were worn thin and
burdened with more children than they had any
good reason to have. The women sort of ran things.
Like a matriarchal society. Like the Novekas are.
Anyway, when they began to trust us it was good.
When I would come to the clinic, four days at a time,
once or twice a month, they would be waiting for me.
It was like seeing my family. It was a good thing," he
repeated with care.

"They started to bring me things although we
asked for no pay. Do you know what they brought,
hombre? Gold. Gold nuggets! Sometimes pieces of
jade. Flakes of silver and the biggest garnets you ever
saw.

"It was not easy or even possible to find out
where they got them. I really never did, but I got a
good idea it was from the old line shock watering
hole you went to. I guess I was right. Anyway, from
around that area. Did you see the dinosaur bones?"

Michael nodded.

"And the ice cave or whatever you call it?"

"Yes, I did. The damnedest thing I ever saw.
There is beer there if you go back yourself. Beer on
ice."

"What?"

"Go see for yourself."

"I probably will, but you asked about Oscar.
Oscar is an asshole we call a coyote. He smuggles

people across the border into the US. He smuggles, I should say he did smuggle, pot and cocaine. He was a big shot son of a bitch in south Texas and northern Mexico. He paid off a lot of authorities in Mexico, which is easy, as you know. Not so easy in the states, but somehow he got to the border patrol guys around McAllen. When the border guys caught some guys trying to get away from Oscar's goons, they found nuggets on them. Nuggets from you know where. Oscar's goons beat it out of them, where they got the gold from the Indians. Some of the people around Oscar, my friends, told me he lit up like a pinball machine. He was a bad man surrounded by bad men before this. Illegals he was supposed to get across the border damn often turned up cooked to death in the freight yards and dead of thirst and dehydration in the desert somewhere. Men, women, children always with their pockets empty, the girls raped. The men beat up and the children left on their own. It was one of the kids who survived who told me about all this at first. I tried to talk to the law, here in Mexico as well as the states. All I got was threats and deaf ears both damn places. It stinks. It really stinks."

Beside being angry by his own words, Pablo looked sad and was close to tears that embarrassed both men.

"Sometimes, señor, men have to take law and punishment into their own hands. It makes our hands bloody like we don't want, but it is the price we must pay." Pablo looked at his hands thoughtfully.